About the Author

Katie Swayne was born and raised in Winston-Salem, North Carolina. She loves baking, reading, and playing board games with her family. She enjoys running with her dad and playing soccer with her brother. Some of her favorite memories are of her mom reading stories to her before bedtime as a child. Katie is incredibly blessed to have such a supportive and loving family.

Dahlia's Kingdom

Katie Swayne

Dahlia's Kingdom

Olympia Publishers
London

www.olympiapublishers.com
OLYMPIA PAPERBACK EDITION

Copyright © Katie Swayne 2024

The right of Katie Swayne to be identified as author of
this work has been asserted in accordance with sections 77 and 78
of the Copyright, Designs and Patents Act 1988.

All Rights Reserved

No reproduction, copy or transmission of this publication
may be made without written permission.
No paragraph of this publication may be reproduced,
copied or transmitted save with the written permission of the
publisher, or in accordance with the provisions
of the Copyright Act 1956 (as amended).

Any person who commits any unauthorized act in relation to
this publication may be liable to criminal
prosecution and civil claims for damage.

A CIP catalogue record for this title is
available from the British Library.

ISBN: 978-1-80439-295-9

This is a work of fiction.
Names, characters, places and incidents originate from the writer's
imagination. Any resemblance to actual persons, living or dead, is
purely coincidental.

First Published in 2024

Olympia Publishers
Tallis House
2 Tallis Street
London
EC4Y 0AB

Printed in Great Britain

Dedication

To Dad, thank you for encouraging me, believing in me, and supporting me as I attempted my first novel. I love you.

Acknowledgements

I'd like to thank my dad, David Swayne, for consistently encouraging me throughout the year that I wrote this novel. He listened patiently to my rants and offered advice, even though I refused to tell him the plot. I'd also like to give a special thank-you to my mom, Gayle, and my brother, Bradley, for loving and supporting me. Since I was born with dyslexia, I would like to thank Kris Cox for teaching me to read, write, and spell during all those years of tutoring lessons. Lastly, I would like to thank God for the wonders He has worked in my life. I certainly would never have written a novel if He had not surrounded me with the people I love the most.

Introduction

I wake up cold. Confused, my eyes flutter open, and I sit up. My back is stiff from lying on the frigid rock.

Quickly, my confusion turns to disbelief, then anger. As questions swirl through my mind, I see the king's face. Firm, determined against all odds, against any obstacle, to kill the only man I've ever loved. Even if it means losing me.

My head hurts from being knocked out and every thought seems to circle slowly in my mind, as if swirling through a stopped-up drain, before finally settling in.

I pinch myself. This can't be real.

Bars in front of me. Solid rock covering the other three walls. Gray everywhere. Even the sky which I can see through the bars.

Chilling winds blow through this dull imprisonment. I shiver.

I glance down. My black dress, which shone so brightly last night, is in tatters. The shawl is gone. One of my heels is cracked and the expensive diamonds that spun upward from my head adorned with ringlets are scattered across the floor.

Shock. Who knows how long I sit here. Staring out the bars. Confused, abandoned, betrayed, afraid.

He's out there right now. Searching for me. I wonder if he'll find me. I wonder if he cares enough to try.

The king seems like a distant memory. I push him away from me with my thoughts. He took everything from me.

I have no thoughts of revenge, no sense of self-righteousness. Just abandonment. A tear drops from my eye as I watch the sun rise on this gray sky.

Curling up into a ball, I rock myself back and forth, fending off the cold. Feeling more alone than ever before. The hollow pit on my stomach craves attention, a human's touch, a kind word.

None is forthcoming from these empty cold walls.

I allow myself a moment more of self-pity before rising to my feet.

Purpose fills my bones as I teeter toward the bars. Time to find a weakness in the king's scheme and exploit it.

I start planning how to open the bars.

2 Years Ago

Chapter 1

When I first met him, I was sitting on a park bench in the middle of town. That boy! I could tell by his eyes that he was worried about being stopped, but so was everyone.

The palace guards were searching for an individual rebel. Some idiot had decided to attack a guard in the bakery. They claimed that they were the rightful ruler of Hazelton, our kingdom. Sigh. People just never understand the burden of ruling.

I wasn't worried about being stopped. I knew the guards couldn't touch me, though they did not know it yet.

I wore a deep burgundy cloak with the hood pulled up, hiding my most prominent features. Long, thick dark brown hair pulled up into an intricate bun. Bright hazel eyes that changed colors. Sometimes bright green, others a deep brown; typically they are a mix, mimicking the forests that inhabit the kingdom. Bright pink lips that did not need makeup to draw attention. My long dark lashes contrasted with my lightly tanned skin.

My fingers traced the lining of the fine fabric. I thought about leaving the square and heading home, but the boy looked downright scared. He spotted me sitting by myself and quickly crossed to the bench.

He could easily be the rebel they were talking about, with his mess of dark hair covered by a hooded cloak that shadowed the rest of his features. He gave me a forced, nervous smile and asked, "Is this seat taken?"

I hesitated for just a second to take him in. He was about six foot, with broad shoulders and an athletic stance. I could probably beat him in hand-to-hand combat if it came down to it, but I had a feeling that he didn't want to make a scene.

"No. Please, sit," I replied.

I gave him a slight smile and scooted over a bit. The bench was a normal metal one with a curved back that had swirls of metal. It was my favorite because it looked toward the swing set that normally had a kid or two chasing each other. Another reminder that I was not to have a normal childhood nor future. I had never been allowed to play with the other children. They always said that it was not appropriate or befitting of my stature and future prospects, though I wholeheartedly disagreed. I always wanted to have the childhood that all the village children had. Even merchants would allow their young children to run and play in their lacy little dresses and miniature suits.

I stopped my wallowing as soon as I realized that the boy was watching me, as if he was waiting for a cue on what to do.

"Good thing we both found each other." He raised an eyebrow. "It's dangerous to be out here alone with rebels running around."

I eyed him. His face was serious but there was a hint of sarcasm in his voice. "Well, we couldn't have that. They would have certainly targeted us," I intoned.

He grinned. "You live around here?"

There were many merchants that came and went in the village. They would come, sell their goods, greet old friends, and leave again, only to return the next year.

I said that I lived a bit outside town, which was not too far from the truth.

He looked at me curiously and stated, "I haven't seen you in the village before."

"I don't come here too often," I replied sharply. It was a simple comment, but it set me on edge. He looked sorry though, and I felt bad for snapping at such a simple comment. In truth, I had never seen him before, which led me to believe that he did not live in the village either.

"Want some ice cream?"

He must be rich to afford a delicacy like that. I responded in the affirmative. No one in their right mind would ever pass up ice cream!

We headed over to the small store on the other side of the square and he bought two vanillas.

"I'm Ash, by the way."

In my hurry not to be identified, I had totally forgotten to introduce myself. He turned to look at me expectantly.

"Dahlia," I said quietly.

He smiled, "I like that name."

We spent the rest of the day together, talking, laughing, and eating. He asked to see me again and I told him I was free next Thursday. We agreed to meet at the iron bench where we first met. When we parted ways, he looked like he wanted to walk me home, but I knew that wasn't an option, so I simply turned to go. He watched me for a minute and turned to go in the other direction.

I saw Ash again that next Thursday and the next. We did not talk much about our lives, where we were from, who our parents were, what schools we went to. It did not bother me. I steered clear of the subject because if I asked the question, he would undoubtedly answer and throw it back at me. And I knew that I could never answer those questions. It did not seem to bother Ash that I never asked about his home life, and he never ventured a question at me.

Having thus omitted that part of our lives from the conversation, we talked about our likes and dislikes. We took walks on the bridge over the river and played games like buruan.

Buruan was a game that town kids played after school. They would take a piece of wood and carve a square board with different shapes inside. After painting a rock red on one side, they would toss the rock onto the board from five feet away. If you landed on one of the symbols, you would get the points for that symbol. But if you landed on the red side of the rock, you would get minus the amount of points. Little kids played it because it worked on their hand-eye coordination. Older kids played it because the winner got to dare somebody to do something. Ash and I played it because it seemed normal and made us laugh.

As I grew to know Ash, I liked him more and more. I knew I would have to tell him who I was eventually, then he would be different…but I liked him the way he was, so for once I let my background be a mystery. I wanted to enjoy these moments and thus I pushed the thoughts to the back of my mind and let them be.

I never wondered why Ash never asked. I was just grateful that he didn't. I assumed he was a normal merchant's child that lived outside the town in some of the richer houses. He never gave me cause to ask about his personal life and he never volunteered the information. Anyway, I knew it was better not to ask.

I trusted Ash more with each passing week. We had many similarities and since we both had impeccable manners and plenty of money to spend, we were able to vary our activities.

We met at our bench every Thursday afternoon for almost a year. It is hard to believe that our first meeting was a year ago plus one week.

Now, dear reader, you are probably wondering who on earth I am; well, the answer should be obvious. I'm a princess, *The* Princess.

Chapter 2

Thwack! The thick iron rod smashes through the air, taking my breath away with pain. I have never known misery of this magnitude. The searing, blinding pain lights my back on fire.

I open my eyes slightly and see Ash standing in the doorway. He locks eyes with me for only a moment, but there is no emotion in them. Neither hatred nor sympathy play where his eyes used to sparkle every time I met them. Where once there was a stream of information, now there is nothing from those deep brown eyes. He is impassive. Not a wisp of the trust and friendship we had built.

Friendship! How could I even think of him in that way? After everything he had done! After all the lies! The hate I feel, the distrust, doesn't seem to compensate for what he has done.

But even then, though I tell myself it is from the beatings and the agony of torture, a small part of me aches for an answer as to why he stands by. That part feels pain but also hope when I see him, and it wonders if any of it was ever real.

Ash turns and walks away. I feel myself start to drown in the pain again. He has not said a word to me this entire time, though he has had plenty of opportunities to try to stop them.

Them being King Samuel Coriander's torturers, who are skilled in extracting every piece of information they can. I have been trained though. I know that I can never speak because every word can be used to hurt someone I love or give something away. I think the king knows this, but he continues with the torture as if he expects me to crack. I will never!

The rod breaks through the air again and a man leans down beside my ear. His voice is hoarse as he whispers, "Anything you would like to share, my lady?"

I bare my teeth at him in response. I know full well that any form of retaliation or resistance will only bring me more pain.

"Fine, one more beating should do it for today." He straightens and nods at the guard who raises the rod and lets it fly.

***

I wake and look around, befuddled, not quite remembering where I am. This is not my room, though it looks like it could be one of the bedrooms near mine.

Then it hits me. The slight sense of security I had vanishes. I am in King Coriander's castle, I am his prisoner, and he wants every scrap of information that I know. He had tried to be civil at first, offering me to lunch and trying to be friendly, but I made it clear that I was not going to be his puppet. He quit the niceties after that.

As I lay in the great bed that is reserved for royal prisoners, I gaze about the room. There is a great crystal chandelier hanging from the ceiling and gold spirals spin out from it like the loopy tendrils of a vine. The walls are dark green and the bedspread a bright yellow that appears to have been spun from pure sunlight.

Most of the time I am treated like a normal prisoner. I sleep in the bed reserved for people like me, eat the food that is prepared, and stay in my room because I am locked in here.

Though it is my prison, I actually enjoy this room. It reminds me of a forest in midsummer. There are no paintings on the walls and only a few plush armchairs to rest in, but my favorite thing about the room is the bookshelf. It is spread across an entire wall and is full of books.

There are books on medicines, hunting, and scientists. Books written about love and war. Even books that have no title and are simply personal diaries of random people that I have never even heard of before.

I also have a closet full of clothes that range from frilly dresses to riding boots to cleaning garbs that look like someone spattered some kind of paint on it in the most random places. These are all at my disposal, but even though they look like they contain some of the finest material in all the land, none of them are close to what I have back home.

Still, I am not going to complain. There could have been much worse clothing situations that I could have imagined.

My back, scabbed and bruised, is finally starting to feel better. The bruises from the beating last week are fading. At least, I think it has been a week. I am judging by the rate of healing, not by time because I have no way to do so.

Originally, I tried to keep a book open and turn one page a day to keep track. They weren't as dumb as I thought, unfortunately. They closed me in a pitch-black holding room for who knows how long until I had no semblance of time, was very bored, and extremely hungry. I stopped trying to keep track after that.

I slip out of bed and head to the closet, where I pull on a simple dark green dress and matching slippers. I have not been allowed to leave my room since the beating so I figure no one will see me. Anyway, I am not planning on impressing anyone here with my outfits.

I pull my hair back into two French braids and grab a book from the bottom shelf. It is, of course, the Holy Book. I start every morning with a chapter and a quick prayer. My parents had taught me their religion and to worship the Great One. I have done this every morning for as long as I can remember.

Today, I read my favorite verse because it discourages fear and tells me to place my trust in the Ancient of Days.

It is comforting to know that He is with me, but sometimes, like now, I feel more alone than ever, with no human interaction and no friends. I refuse to let myself dive down that rabbit hole of self-pity though.

After praying, I dive straight into Shakespeare's *Merchant of Venice*. Personally, I prefer *The Tempest*, but I have already read that twice in the past week and feel I should read something else if I am going to read Shakespeare.

After about an hour of struggling over iambic pentameter and blank verse, a knock comes at the door. It is followed by half a dozen guards barging into the room, swords at the ready. I turn peacefully. In my mind, I smile because if I wanted to, I could take out those guards like a piece of cake. Navigating my way out of the castle would be another problem though and I would rather not show my hand that quickly.

Two approach me and force me to stand. Binding my wrists together, they guide me out of the room and down the wide hallway equipped with suits of armor at every doorway. Or are they people? I can't tell because they are so still, and the helmet covers their entire face.

I am escorted, or should I say shoved, into another, grander, room with large windows that face out over a picturesque garden.

"Sit," grunts one of the guards behind me.

I do as directed, and they back off me for a minute, standing guard by the doorway behind me. Silence follows, broken only by the light breathing of the guards and the shuffling of their heavy boots.

"Why didn't you tell me?"

I am startled to hear the voice behind me; I did not even hear him enter. The even greater surprise comes to me as I realize that I know that voice.

Ash.

A thousand thoughts rush through my head as I wonder what he wants with me. He clearly played me well by getting to know me, pretending to be normal, and then targeting me, a girl who simply wanted friendship. I would have never guessed that the Ash from the village that I knew was the same Grand Prince Ashton Coriander from Tamar, the kingdom beside ours. From the same Coriander family that is on the brink of war with ours. The shock of this discovery, along with the distress of being torn from my family, nearly brings me to tears.

Instead, I clasp my quivering hands together neatly in my lap and reply with clever coolness, "The same reason you didn't tell me, I suppose."

He's quiet for a moment and then directs his next orders to the guards, "Leave us."

Well, of all the things he would request from the guards, that wasn't even on the list, and it was a long one. Filled with torture for me while he tried to make me spill the secrets that his father had failed to retrieve.

The guards file out of the room, but I don't turn my head. I don't want to see him. He stands there and I feel his eyes on my back, watching me. Finally, he crosses to a chair opposite me.

I can't help glancing up to see the look on his face. By the look of it, he seems to be trying to make a decision. I watch him stare at the chair as if deciding to sit or not.

Then, he surprises me again by pulling a knife from his pocket and I am wondering why I even let myself think that he might still care about me when he slices through the ropes binding my hands together.

Wow, it hasn't even been a full minute since that last surprise. Does he even know how deadly I am? I was expecting him to fulfil the torture himself. To take revenge for the fact that I never told him who I was.

Maybe he thinks that he can take me. I think that it would be a pretty fair fight, especially since he has a knife, but I have fought the best of the best. I could beat him eventually.

My father made sure that I was trained in the fine arts of death. I have never actually had to kill someone, but I know about a hundred different ways to do it.

I have finally decided where to strike first when he says, "I wouldn't do that if I were you, Dahlia. My father already wants you dead. It's been all I can do to even keep you alive."

Okay, so maybe this is another interview tactic, because he has been way too nice in these last few minutes. Sure, he was kind in the village. If he was still the Ash from the village, I would not question his motives nor the fact that he would fight his father to keep me alive.

But this is not the Ash I know. So, what to make of this comment? Should I trust that some form of the village Ash is still in there, or is this a ploy? What to say...what to say. My mind has forgotten how to form the sentences that are nearly always on the tip of my tongue.

Also, how did he just know that I was preparing to kill him? He was in the process of sitting down in a chair. I decide to make that a priority because I should not be so easy to read.

"And what exactly am I not doing?" I raise an eyebrow with my question.

He just laughs, and then, smiling, says, "Trying to kill me."

Well, there we go; he knew exactly what I was going to do. I wonder why he finds me killing him so humorous.

"How did you know that?"

"Dahlia, let's just say that I've spent enough Thursdays watching you to know that you were about to pounce."

I simply raise an eyebrow again. It says what I won't. Explain.

"Your face doesn't show a sign, don't worry." He is still smiling, and it bothers me. "Your shoulders lean forward and your hands, which you have kept neatly in your lap this entire time, have tensed. All in all, you are much better than most people."

I think he means to compliment me, but I am lost in the fact that he saw the slightest tension of the muscles in my fingertips. Odd.

"Remarkable." The word escapes my lips before I can stop it. I would have said that to village Ash. I need to remember that this is a different person. We are not just wandering through the village and eating fresh apples. He is interrogating me, and I am trying to not reveal anything about myself. All I'm aware of is that he already knows too much.

"Why did you sneak into the village? You could have easily gone as yourself. Everyone loves you."

His words seem to float to me through a thick fog and I just want to run, to escape. I know too much about my kingdom, too much about my parents, too many plans that are being enacted or are in the making. I can't tell him any of it, yet part of me still feels like I can trust him, like he is still my friend. But I'm just lying to myself.

"I don't like the attention." A harmless answer that contains part of the reason. The other reason being that my parents would never allow me to travel to the village alone. Because the unthinkable might happen. And now it has.

He just watches me. His eyes searching mine. He knows that is not the answer, but he doesn't press me. I try to keep my face steady, but I know that the cracks will start to show soon.

Especially since I am so close to someone that I know so well. Just a few weeks ago, I would have happily defended Ash with my life if he was threatened.

Now, I'm not sure what I'd do.

"What are you thinking about, Dahlia?" His voice is gentle, like he actually cares. Only, I know better. This false gentleness brings me out of my stupor. Why can't I just treat him like any of my other captors? He seems to care, but he has clearly lied to me many times about his life. It wouldn't surprise me if he was lying now. Toying with my heart like he has for a year.

"None of your business, Ash," I retort with none of the usual kindness that used to linger on my every syllable. Now I am harsh.

"I should have told you," he says quietly. "I really thought that you were from the village. I figured you would turn me in to the guards and that I would be sent to the palace dungeons. I couldn't risk that."

I feel vulnerable in my slippers. My slim dress barely reaches the tops of my knees. I briefly wonder what my father would say if he could see me looking like this, talking with the heir of the enemy. A slight shiver runs down my spine and I glance up at Ash to make sure he has not seen the homesick tears well up in my eyes. It would not do to appear weak.

Ash has turned his head away from me, looking over the back of his chair out the window. I barely catch his next words, but they grow in strength as he speaks.

"I was so shocked when I saw you in that carriage. My job was to attack the royal palace carriage traveling through Hazelton. We had received rumors that the Grand Princess Elowyn Dayana Wisteria would be traveling in it. I didn't know that she went by Dahlia." He rises and walks to stand by the window, "By the time that I recovered from my shock at seeing you in the overturned carriage and believed that my eyes weren't deceiving me, it was too late. You were in custody, and I couldn't defy direct orders from my father. Anyway, he sent the very best to trap you. I would have been killed trying and you would already be dead."

My resolve not to believe him is quickly dissolving. It seems that while I have been planning my escape and his murder, he has been working just as hard to save my life. He seems to be telling the truth and I do not know what to believe.

"Why should I trust you?" My voice betrays me with a slight quaver. Anyone who knows me would be able to tell that my stubborn, resolute, obstinate mind is teetering back and forth. This is very unfortunate because Ash knows me better than almost anyone.

He turns to look at me from the window and his eyes are his own as he speaks. They are no longer the impassive brick walls that have been guarded from me. They look hurt by the question, sad to see that I no longer trust him completely, and determined to win back that trust.

"Because I would never do anything to hurt you. Because I will keep you as safe as I can at all costs. Because you're my friend."

I watch him, impassive, trying to find a chink in his statement, a way out of his claim, but none comes to me.

"What do I need to do?" I'm thrown off guard by the question. He genuinely seems to be willing to do anything.

I retaliate with a question of my own. "Why have you watched me beaten a dozen different ways, too many times to count, and never spoken a word?"

"Because my father would find out," he answers. "If he had any idea that I cared even the slightest bit about you, he would do so many worse things to you. He would exploit every weakness and every person that you have ever loved."

"Why?"

"Because one thing that he can't stand more than not succeeding in getting information out of you is me falling in love with someone like you."

"Someone like me. What's that supposed to mean?" The words feel like they should hurt, but the way Ash says it, he makes me feel like I'm special. Also, did he just say falling in love? The farthest I would go is to say that we are friends and, after everything he's done, even that is stretching it at this point.

"Someone who is an enemy to our country. Yet every other trait about them is perfect. "They are kind, smart, and wealthy. They are the heir to their throne and have a large, prosperous kingdom. He can't find a solid argument against you besides the fact that you are the daughter of Queen Amore and King Javor. Even that is not a good enough reason, because he knows that it would be a good thing if I married you."

Married me! Where did that come from? I know that one day I will have to marry and pass on the family name, create an heir, but we're seventeen! I'm not even Queen of Hazelton yet and may not be for some time.

My eyes must have shown the shock I was feeling because Ash makes an effort to reassure me.

"Dahlia, please don't get me wrong, I'm not proposing. I was just explaining why it would be bad for my father to know that I like you. That we are friends." He pauses his quick response and seems to be asking me with his eyes if we are still friends.

Here is my chance; I could verify his claim to my friendship or I could dash it and destroy any hopes of having a person who might help me get out of here. Anyway, it couldn't hurt to play along and part of me knows that even if he tried to kill me, I would still call him my friend. I know him too well to push him away like that.

"Of course, we're friends," I say.

He smiles and comes to stand in front of me. "I'll do my best to get you out of here and keep my father away. I promise." I know that he needs to leave soon before anyone gets suspicious.

I nod. I'm not ready to completely trust him. I don't expect him to keep his promise, but he has given me some hope. And I desperately need some hope, so I allow myself to trust him, if just for the moment.

I think that he understands because he gives me a smile, squeezes my shoulder, and walks toward the door. Just as he reaches the handle, I turn. "Thank you, Ash." It is all I can say at the moment. My throat seems to have squeezed in on itself. He pauses, then turns the handle and walks out the door.

Chapter 3

In my dreams, I am fighting one of my trainers. Most people would scoff at the thought of training a princess how to fight but my parents are determined to keep me safe, not only because I am heir to the throne but also because I am their child. If teaching me to kill keeps me from being killed, they will seek out the best to teach me, which they did.

My opponent carries a long knife. We circle each other on the field. I am weaponless as always. It would be too unfair an advantage to give me so much as a knife. I would easily throw it and, as always, it would find his heart. Of course, I would never kill someone in training.

Anyway, the battle would be over too quickly if I did that.

He attacks and I duck, avoiding the slicing sword. He knows that I am fast enough to avoid his blade. As he moves past me, I drive my elbow into the back of his knee. He stumbles but does not fall.

He moves back into position. I am on the balls of my feet, waiting for the attack. He tries to strike low this time and as I catapult myself over the blade, I wrap my legs around his neck and use my momentum to flip him onto the ground. Immediately, before he has time to recover, I hold his arm down with my foot and jerk the sword from his hand.

Holding the knife to his throat, I hear my father call out, "Twelve seconds. Stop playing around. You should have gotten him the first time."

I scowl and rise to my feet, freeing my trainer. He rises, gives me a slight thumbs up and suggests we do archery. Good, I love archery. I can hit the bullseye every time with an arrow, knife, and sword.

You name it, I can kill with it. As I go to pull back the drawstring, something feels wrong. I turn and suddenly, I am in the forest again. My carriage travels down the path. I hear the battle going on outside and prepare myself to fight. The carriage tips and I tumble around in it, feeling like nothing more than a sack of flour being tossed this way and that. As the carriage comes to a stop, I grab my knife that I have hidden under the layers of my skirt. I turn and bend my knees, ready to launch myself at the first enemy to open my door.

The door opens and I falter; Ash looks just as shocked as I feel, seeing him in a prince's garb, knowing that he clearly attacked me. I am confused for just for a second, but that was enough to let me be captured. The arms grabbed me and tied my hands, hoisting me out of the carriage. I turn to glance back at Ash, still confused by what is happening, wondering how he could do this to me, but it is no longer Ash who stands there. A long dark face with deep set eyes and pursed lips stares back at me. The same face that has watched every torture that I have experienced in this awful palace.

Ash's father, King Samuel Coriander, smiles at my fear and takes a lunging step my way.

I wake, gasping for air, unsure why he scares me so much. It seems like he enjoys watching me scream.

***

It has been three days since I spoke with Ash. He has kept his word and I have not seen the king since the beating approximately a week and a half ago. I wonder what he said to make his father leave me alone for so long.

It is boring, though; I miss being outside, running, riding, playing in the hilly fields that lay just outside of the palace walls. Mostly, I miss the fresh air, the breeze on my skin, the smell of wind in a forest.

My room has a small window that looks out into the palace courtyard. I can watch people go to and fro but it is locked and I know that I will never be allowed to open it. I have finished reading all the Shakespeare books on the shelf and have started on a stranger's diary. I think they may have been someone who was imprisoned here. I doubt that they would keep a book about a prisoner from here, but you never know. They have just written about their thoughts, but that is enough to tell me that they are going through some kind of isolation.

A crash in the hallway breaks me from my thoughts. It sounds as if a whole tray of china was dropped. For a moment, I feel pity for the servant who just lost their job but then I stop myself. Anyone who works for a king like King Samuel must be a terrible person.

As someone begins to yell in the hallway, the door opens slightly. Ash slides through the door and closes it quietly behind him.

"Hey," he whispers.

"Hi," I respond shortly, placing my book on the side table.

"How are you holding up?" His face is genuinely concerned. He is not making it easy for me to distrust him.

"A little bored but otherwise fine," I say with a shrug.

What else am I supposed to tell him? It's not like anything interesting has happened in the past few weeks.

"My father won't leave you alone for much longer. I convinced him to come with me on a hunting trip for the past few days, but we just got back and he was already talking to me about how else we could torture you to make you crack." He looks down at the ground. "I'm really sorry."

Well, I knew that this peace wouldn't last forever.

Although I know exactly how to crack me, I could never tell Ash, not after knowing who his parents are.

"No, it's really okay." I try to make my voice gentle. "You did the best you could and I'm grateful."

He lifts his eyes from the rug and gives me a small smile that looks like a grimace. "Dahlia, is there anything you could tell me so I could show my father that peaceful sessions work?"

My eyes widen at the very thought. "You want me to tell you important information about my kingdom so you can tell your father? Isn't that the whole reason I am being tortured, because I won't talk?" Really. How can he even fantasize with that idea? He should know that I will never talk.

"Sorry, I had to ask. I just wish I could find a way to get him to let me try diplomacy. Then he would leave you alone if he thought it was working."

I quirk an eyebrow. "He will never leave me alone. Eventually, I will have nothing left to tell you and he will torture me to death trying to get information I don't have."

Ash looks so sad and helpless. His eyes fall again to the rug. I know that he wants to help, but at the same time, he was the one who captured me in the first place. I am trying to reconcile the fact that he kidnapped me with the fact that he had no idea and now is trying to help.

"I'll see what I can do." He glances over his shoulder toward the door. The screaming has stopped, and they seem to be cleaning the floor. "I need to go before anyone realizes I am in here."

Ash reaches in his inside jacket pocket and places a deck of cards on the small table. "For you," he whispers. Then Ash turns on his heel and walks out the door.

Chapter 4

How did he know? I had played many card games in my life but only at the castle in Hazelton. They were a rarity and a luxury only the best could afford. I could never have brought a deck to the town. Ash would immediately have suspected something. That was probably why he had never brought one either. Both of us would have known that the other was either royalty or a thief.

I toy with the deck, turning it over and over in my hands. I guess it wouldn't be hard to guess that, as a princess, I had probably seen one before. Still, paper was expensive and the thick cards with the intricate designs of kings and queens must have cost a fortune.

As I flip one of them over, I see a unique crown of jewels that the queen of diamonds wears on her golden curls. It reminds me of another crown. My mother's.

She rarely wears it, preferring the more delicate ones that should belong to children. Her official crown is a rich gold with emeralds and sapphires that match her eyes.

Long ago, when I was younger, I remember asking her about it once. I was getting my crown out of the royal vault. Officially, I was supposed to have a procession of guards bring it to me, but I had begged my mother to let me get it myself. Partially because I wanted to do something for myself for a change and partially because I wanted to see all the other royal jewels.

My mother had agreed to bring me herself and she was going to obtain her crown while down there. As I gazed around at the royal jewels, I noticed that not a single one of the royal jewels looked anything like the ones that my mother normally wore. All of them were bulky and large. They had gaudy bejeweled spikes that looked like they weighed more than me. They were beautiful, but compared to my mother's, I thought they were a bit obsessive and over the top.

My mother retrieved the queen's crown from a red cushion and turned to a mirror that was set in the wall. The crown looked stunning on her, but it didn't match the mother I knew. My mother wore small, intricate, beautifully designed jewelry.

She always had a dainty look about her. If a person did not know her, they would think that a gust of wind might blow her over. She was a normal height, but her slight frame made most people think she was sickly. How else would a rich queen look so much like a commoner?

But her similarities to the townspeople stopped there. Her rich blue-green eyes, flecked with gold, sparkled like the sun on the peaks of the ocean, her smile made men stop in their tracks and stare, and her voice was clear and warm, like the spring. She was a woman of her own mind, unlike most of the day.

When she had an opinion, she expressed it, all the while making you feel like yours was extremely important as well. She was honest, but not rude, smart, but not demeaning, and firm, but not unwilling to learn.

While most queens faded into their husband's shadow, my mother stood by his side.

When the world said a queen was meant to show the king's power by the standard of their beauty, my mother made everything around her shine as well.

So, as I stood looking at the jewels around me, I asked, "Why do you never wear your crown, Mommy?"

It was such a beautiful masterpiece, and she could pull it off. If she wore that instead of her modest, dainty crowns, she would easily outshine everyone in the room. And as queen, it was my six-year-old understanding that every queen should be seen as the most beautiful and admired.

"Are you asking about my crown because you think it would make me prettier?"

I nodded.

"Well, chérie, it isn't about beauty. I know I am pretty. I do not need to show it off. I prefer being in the shadows, watching instead of taking up the spotlight."

I still don't understand. She could be the envy of every kingdom. My confusion shows on my face. I haven't had the face lessons yet where I learned to wipe every emotion from my face.

"I don't need people to want to be like me. I want to build others up, not make them jealous." Her voice is as gentle as ever.

Finally, I get it. My little, insecure six-year-old mind grasps the fact that being beautiful isn't everything. I reach up and retrieve my miniature crown. My mother had it made specially for me as a baby. It is full of twisting silver with tiny leaves that sparkle with emeralds and light pink rubies. Nestled in my brown hair, which is styled up in ringlets, the crown truly looks like a green vine in the forest, traced with sunlight and blooming with flowers.

I love it. It looks more like my mother than my father but after my conversation with her, I agree. I prefer simple and delicate too.

I turn to look out my window in the Coriander palace; there is not a single delicate piece in the whole court. Solo rocks and carts are strewn about, and the walls are rough stone, their bulky weight providing a natural defense against invasion.

The inside parts of the castle are nice enough, though I haven't had much to judge by. My castle is picturesque, with winding towers and green vines. The landscape is filled with gardens and flowers blooming in every color imaginable. The Corianders' castle has not been influenced by my mother's art and therefore looks like a pile of undesirable rock, piled into a fortress.

As I flip through the cards, I notice one has been bent slightly. Odd. Most decks are treasured and dealt with carefully. I know that I was given one for my tenth birthday by the King of Regne. All the decks in my home were treasured and cared for with the utmost attention.

My father had his own airtight container designed specially to hold the few decks that we owned. I feel like the Corianders would care for their decks as well. Even though the outside of the castle walls looks hideous, the inside is well cared for. They do not lack for money and seem to care for their own possessions, if not for the rest of their kingdom.

I go back to inspecting the card. It is an ace of hearts. As I flip over the card, I see it. In the bottom right-hand corner, a tiny inscription.

Want to get out?

Chapter 5

A trick most likely. But also something that Ash could never say in person because of the danger of being overheard. He could be convicted of treason for this simple line.

I know that it might be a trap, but it also might be my only chance to go home.

I don't know enough about the castle to get out on my own. If I knew the layout or had a guide, I could easily fight my way out.

But he could also be leading me straight to his father. Or he could be trying to get me to trust him. Either way, I do not have enough information to make an educated decision. Every single part of my training has instructed me to never, ever, trust a person in another castle. All my instructors would grimace if they even knew that I was considering the possibility.

My training has always been with the idea of a stranger in mind or somebody that I have met during my captivity. Nothing has prepared me for the possibility of knowing the person before my captivity.

First my acquaintance, our growth to friendship, then his betrayal, his attempts at reconciliation, and now his offer. I trusted this boy, before I knew that he had hid himself from me. That he was coming to the village to gain information as a spy. That his goal was to capture a member of the royal family.

But Ash said he didn't know I was royalty. I don't believe

him, not yet. There is too much evidence that points to the contrary.

And yet, just maybe, he might want to help me. I remember the look in his eyes, as he opened the carriage door. So ready to fight and then utter confusion and shock. It could be acting, or it could be genuine. I might never know.

My brain gets so clouded when I think about all the possibilities of why Ash claims to wish to get me out. He seems to want to help, and at the same time, he is the reason I am here. I know all my training points to not trusting him, but every time I look at him, I see the boy from the village. My friend. Yet, somehow, he is the son of my father's mortal enemy.

I think that may be why King Samuel loves torturing me. Just because he feels like my screams will somehow make their way to my father and wound him.

They used to be friends, Samuel and my father. They grew up in the same social circle of royalty and lived in kingdoms beside each other. Both heirs to their individual throne, they hosted balls and parties every month, looking for a wife. At one of the many balls, Samuel met a beautiful girl named Amore Cariad. She was the daughter of Abakire, the second prince of the kingdom Saibhir.

A princess, although not directly in line for the throne, Amore won the hearts of many at that ball. Unfortunately, with her bright rosy cheeks and dazzling smile, she also won both the princes' hearts. Samuel courted her for several months while my father watched on, miserably.

One evening, Samuel decided to share his plans about how he was going to change his kingdom once he became king. Unfortunately, he did not share the information about how he was going to hire doctors for all of his people, or his intentions to create peace between the warring countries in the South. Instead, he shared his thoughts about how he would limit women from going to social gatherings. His belief was that women should only leave the house when absolutely necessary. They should stay with the children and give men some freedom to roam about without them.

He went on to explain that he was going to bring back the tradition of having multiple wives. He felt it would better prepare his offspring for being royalty if they had more competition among their siblings.

After his speech, during which Amore sat speechless with horror and disgust, Samuel got down on one knee and proposed. Naturally, Amore wanted nothing to do with Samuel after he confessed that he was going to marry multiple wives and oppress women.

She went on one of the very few tirades of her life. Samuel was expecting support from his amiable girlfriend, instead he received criticism. In that moment of frustration, he made another error. He struck Amore. It can easily be said that that was the last straw for Amore.

Amore left Samuel and made it very clear she wanted nothing to do with him ever again. But when she left, she had nowhere to go, for she had been staying at the castle during their courtship.

The closest person she knew was my father, in the neighboring kingdom. She knew he was close friends with Samuel but trusted him not to reveal her.

Unfortunately, Amore was seen entering the palace in Hazelton and word got back to Samuel. In return, Samuel cut off his relationship and all communication with my father.

Obviously, this caused my father to question Amore about what had happened the previous night. She explained Samuel's perspective. While doing so, Amore and my father realized they had much in common. My father started courting Amore and she stayed as an honored guest in the palace.

One day, a letter arrived from Samuel. It requested that Amore be brought to the castle in Tamar, Samuel's kingdom. He had permission from Abakire, Amore's father, to make her his wife.

My father ignored the letter and continued his courtship of Amore. Unlike Samuel, my father informed Amore about the letter, though he refused to let that be her fate. They spent time together for a few months and the letter was forgotten.

One day, in late spring, my father asked Amore to marry him. She accepted. They proclaimed the news throughout the whole kingdom. Everyone celebrated because Amore had a kind heart and was loved by all the people.

Well, everyone besides Samuel. His rage at my father's betrayal caused him to fulfill all that he had promised to enforce on women and more. He would never allow a woman to make a decision that men did not approve of again. He had learned his lesson.

In the meantime, my father and Amore, who you have probably guessed is my mother by now, were married. They worked together to improve and strengthen the kingdom. My mother and father were loved by all, whereas Samuel was despised.

The two boys who grew up as best friends became bitter enemies. My father could never forgive Samuel for his intentions with my mother and Samuel could never forgive my father for choosing Amore over himself.

Thus, when I scream, I believe that he feels that he is justifying himself against my father's 'wrongs'.

I settle back into my chair, looking at the cards. I study every inch of every card but none of the others have been touched.

So, the question remains, do I want to get out? I need to focus on that but, to answer that question, I need to answer another one first.

Do I trust Ash?

Chapter 6

I wake to see a tall dark figure standing over me. It is still in the early hours of the morning and the sun has not yet risen. The man holds a finger to his lips and gestures for me to rise. I slip out of bed in nothing but a thin nightgown that barely reaches my knees. I had not expected a guest.

He looks me once over and again gestures with his hand but this time toward the closet. He has not shown intentions of being hostile, but then again, he is in my room in the middle of the night. I try to get a glimpse of his face, but it is obscured by the black fabric that covers him from head to toe. There seem to be slits for the eyes, but I cannot be sure in the dark.

Feeling strangely calm, I walk to the closet, enter, and close the door after me. I pick out a dark green blouse and flowing black pants. I had not noticed how colorful everything in the closet was until now.

I reemerge into my room, my eyes finally adjusting to the darkness. Still, it is hard to see anything. The stranger is no longer standing beside my bed. In fact, he is nowhere to be seen. I notice a movement out of the corner of my right eye just as his hand closes over my mouth.

I stifle a scream. His grip is tight and I cannot break it. I struggle as he turns me, pressing my back against the wall. His voice is gruff as he hisses, "Follow my lead. Don't make a sound."

He releases his hold on me, turns, and glides toward the door. His footfalls are soundless, and he moves so smoothly that you can almost imagine he had wheels for feet.

My heart is beating to the rhythm of the quickstep. I take a deep breath and try to think but my head is foggy from being unable to breathe. Who is he? What does he want? Where is he taking me? And thousands of similar questions flood through my head. I can't think straight.

I look up and see him looking back at me from the doorway. I take a moment to steady myself and follow this mysterious stranger into the dark castle corridors.

***

Right, left, up one staircase, and down another. I am completely lost. I have no semblance of direction and no clue where I am. It feels like we have been walking for at least an hour.

My strange guide seems very confident about where he is going, almost like he has rehearsed this path hundreds of times. We pass cleaning closets and guest rooms, sitting areas and fencing classrooms. I feel like I am walking in circles. I could swear that we had passed that room with the green door before, but who knows, there could be hundreds of rooms with green doors in this place.

My span of knowledge of the castle consists of my room, the corridor beyond, and the route to the dungeon. Very helpful.

Still, I haven't seen a single guard this whole time. Therefore, he must be doing something right. I know guards pass the corridor outside my door every five minutes. He must have extensive knowledge of the castle if he can manage to avoid the guards. They seem to be constantly swarming every part of the castle.

Also, my door is normally locked. I wonder how he managed that. Another thing to add to the list of questions growing in my head.

I am so wrapped up in my thoughts that I don't notice the stranger has stopped. He anticipates my forward movement and turns slightly, placing a hand on my shoulder, as he peers around the corner. I wonder what made him stop.

Then I hear it. It must be a very long corridor because the sound is faint, but I am fairly sure there are two people talking at the end of the hall. By the tone of their voices, I would guess there are two guards conversing, though we are too far away to hear what they are discussing.

The stranger takes a few glances around at the surrounding doors and pulls me by the arm into one of the rooms. He motions for me to remain there and slips back into the hallway.

I am left alone to my thoughts for a minute and for the first time I consider the consequences of my actions. Sure, I followed this man because of the possibility that he might be helping me escape. But what if he is leading me into a trap? Is Samuel behind this? If so, why would the guards be in our way, to win my trust? Samuel does not need me to do anything to have ample reason to kill me.

I hear a thud. By the sound of it, someone is on the ground. There is a sound of a light struggle and I hear a second thud. Well, this would lead me to assume that my strange guide is also a skilled assassin.

The door opens and the stranger motions for me to follow

him. The guards are nowhere to be seen. I wonder what he did with them. He certainly took them out pretty fast.

I try to remember the route that we take but there are so many turns. Right, left, around a corner, backtrack down a hall, up two flights of stairs, through a servants' door, down a flight of stairs, back out into the hallway. I am sure that it must be almost daylight when the stranger opens a door to… the armory? I thought we were getting out, not arming ourselves. I must have a questioning look on my face because he gives me a little shake of his head: *not now*.

My questions stick in the back of my throat, but I have trusted him this far. I step into the chamber and grab a sword and sheath, which I wrap around my waist. I slide a set of arrows over my head and grab a bow. I turn to see that my guide has not been idle. He is loaded up with his own set of arrows, a bow, a sword, and something that looks like the mix between a sword and an exaggerated saw. The length is like a sword, but instead of a smooth blade ending on one side with a lethal edge, the edge of this weapon has a zigzag pattern with curves at the end of each point.

He points to a row of daggers. Does he think we will need all of this to break out? I thought he was good enough to get past the guards. I slide one into the outside of each of my boots and slide an extra one on the inside of each just in case. I turn and follow the stranger out the door. He locks it and slips the key back into his pocket. Then, we head back into the maze of corridors.

***

I am seriously considering just trying to go out a window when we reach another door.

There are windows in every room we pass. We could be shot trying to escape out of one of them, though. And, despite my doubts, this stranger has still managed to avoid all the guards but two. I just feel like we could have escaped by now.

There is a smell in this part of the palace that I cannot place. It has been so long since my senses have been put to use that they are rusty. I know this scent should be easy to identify because I have the sense of smelling it every day when I was at home.

The stranger produces another key and turns the lock. The door swings open, and I feel like smacking the heel of my palm to my forehead.

We are in the stable.

Manure. How could I have missed a smell like that? So easily identifiable and yet it evaded my grasp until I saw it with my own eyes.

Two beautiful chocolate brown mares are standing outside their stalls. They are already saddled, their bridles tied to the posts. Their heads turn toward us when we enter.

The stranger moves swiftly toward the horses, unties the bridle of one, and hoists himself into the saddle. I follow closely behind. The minute I am settled into the seat, he starts walking his horse out of the stable. I stay to the right of him and slightly behind, waiting for him to show me where to go.

It seems strange to me that we are walking out of the stable in plain sight. In the palace, my guide was careful with every step. He peered around every corner, never made a sound, and checked his shoulder by the second.

The stranger still seems extremely alert, and of course my senses are heightened as well, but he seems too casual at this moment.

We reach the door of the stable, and he turns to look at me. I cannot see his eyes underneath all of his black, furrowing garments. His face is still hidden from me. I have a strange urge to reach over and pull up his mask, but he is wearing it for a reason, and for the moment, I will respect that. He has gotten me this far.

He nods toward the door and turns, taking an arrow from his back and fitting it to the bowstring. So, we must fight to get out; no wonder he stopped being so careful once we reached this point.

Samuel obviously must have the entrances and exits well guarded. I feel a new sense of anxiety wash over me, different from the sneaking around. I am well used to both forms of movement because of my training, but I have been locked in my room for weeks. I know it should be instinct, yet I still worry. Rarely have I actually had to use my training. This is the moment where it will count though.

I fit an arrow to my own bowstring, holding on to the horse with my thighs by instinct and using my feet to steer. Hopefully, King Samuel had the good sense to train his horses with the best trainers. Soon I will find out.

My guide spurs his horse through the door and I follow, turning to find the guards with my arrows before they find me with theirs.

Chapter 7

Arrows fly down all around me. We are fish in a barrel in the courtyard. Spotting them hiding in the towers, I let arrow after arrow fly. I only need one for each guard, but there are so many. I find their heads; every guard has holes for the eyes, and I have spent much of my time shooting in the dark.

I watch them topple, one after another, off of the parapets of their respective towers. I have been doing this since I was five. There is no difficulty in this exercise except for the fact that they are trying to kill me, which is actually a big difference. I reload another arrow. A horn blows, this place will be overrun in minutes.

I glance over at my stranger and see him sending arrow after arrow into the battlements, but the men do not fall. Strange, he seems to be aiming right for their chest. Then I realize the brilliant accuracy this person has, it could rival mine with a few tweaks. I send three more arrows at the guards to my right.

The stranger is not aiming to kill, as I have been trained, but to disable. He hits every person in their right arm, severing the ligament in their shoulder. They will live, but never be able to shoot again. I am interested. Why would he care about these guards with their brutality and loyalty to an evil king? But, as long as there is one less guard trying to kill me, I am satisfied.

The horn blows again. I locate the blower this time and send an arrow straight through his skull. It is too late. The whole castle knows we are here. I turn to see my stranger riding toward the wall. Urging my horse forward, I follow. We have bought ourselves a few seconds of peace with our excellent shooting.

Really, it was an excellent round; every arrow hit the mark exactly. I see a small door in the side of the wall that my stranger is aiming for. We are nearly there. Other soldiers are entering from the side of the castle to our left. They are closer to the door. If they get there before us, they will disable our horses and overwhelm us with their massive numbers in minutes. I won't go down fast, but I will go down with the sheer force of hundreds, all fighting to bring me down.

My guide barrels forward, nearly there, nearly there. For a second, I realize the door is closed. Guards are hurtling toward us, almost, almost, and we are through. Rushing past the guards' thrust-out swords by inches, the stranger's horse hits the door at full force. The door swings wide open and I follow right on his heels.

The cool breeze the courtyard lacked hits my face and I take a deep breath. I have not smelled the morning air in weeks. I know there are other guards behind. They will chase us. There were plenty of horses to go around. But we have a solid head start. We will make it to the border of the kingdom before they catch us.

I glance back over my shoulder, turning my body slightly to the right. The arrow slips past my twisted shoulder, just missing me, and hits my guide in the back. He crumples forward on his horse, barely managing to hang on.

As his horse slows, I increase my horse's speed to come beside him. He is alive, barely. I cannot see his skin, but the arrow appears to have landed on the left side in the middle of his back. So spleen, pancreas, or stomach. If it is his pancreas or stomach, there is not much I can do. He has time, though he is in severe pain.

"Can you hold on?"

At this close range, I can finally see his eyes. The skin around them is taunt and his eyes show pain, but he nods. I wonder for a moment if he can actually hold on. Then I question myself. Am I really willing to risk my escape for this stranger? He might already be as good as dead depending on what that arrow hit. But am I capable of leaving this person behind after all he has done for me? The answer, for better or worse, is no. My compassion wins out, though I would never admit it. He saved my life by helping me escape, I tell myself. I owe him this.

My personal exchange with myself lasts approximately half a second. I reach over, grab the reins of his horse, and tie them to my saddle. Then, I ride toward the border at a full gallop, hoping that we can reach my kingdom before Samuel's guards reach us.

Chapter 8

I raise my arms in an X above my head, immediately straighten them horizontally to the sides, then raise my right arm straight up, keeping my left arm out to the side. I hold the position for a moment, then I return my arms to the X position above my head and repeat the sequence. The guards about five miles inside the border of Hazelton should be able to see me in the dark.

The signals will allow me to reach them safely. Though simple, they are only for the royal family. Easily copied, yet they give us another slight advantage, and at this moment, I am very grateful for my father's extra safety measures. It is still dark, so I would have been shot on sight.

The guards are very careful. Especially at the border of Tamar.

I slow to a trot, then a walk. The stranger has managed to hang on. I left the arrow in his back because it stops the blood flow and, if we stopped, he might have given up. Also, I do not want to look at the wound. It will be best to bring him to my father at the palace. He can fix this.

The guard slowly approaches the side of my horse, hand on the hilt of his sword.

Multiple archers line the top of the guard post, arrows already on the bowstring. I remember that I have been riding for two hours with my bow in hand in case anyone manages to follow us.

I look into the guard's face, then reach up gently and lower my hood, displaying my face.

The guard staress suspiciously up at me and then calls for a lantern.

I do not have time for this. Even riding at a full gallop, it has been too long since the stranger was shot. He was my guide. I need him to live. There are so many questions I need answered. If he dies, what will I do? I owe him my freedom. I should be helping him, not sitting by this post waiting for the guards to decide if I can pass.

As the light falls on the guard's face, I recognize him. He is not one of the guards I see often, but he is of a higher rank so he visits the castle periodically. He gives reports to my father. Sometimes I have sat in and listened.

"No, I do not have any royal symbols, rings, or clothes." It is standard procedure to check our signet rings before allowing a border cross. "I need to get him to the castle. Now."

"I need proof of identification first, madame." Really? This man was dying.

"Well, that might be hard, since I have been imprisoned in Tamar for the last few weeks." I know I should play this smart, but my frustration and impatience is getting the better of me. I don't have time. And if I don't have time, then I must not waste it.

With this in mind, I spur my horse, making her rear and dart forward a few steps. I turn and shoot the lantern. The gas explodes.

All but two of the archers are either blown to their knees or are running down the stairs to their friend.

I feel slight remorse, but I do not have time to worry. The soldier will live.

I take a note from my guide's book and shoot the remaining two guards in the shoulder, between the armor. Then, I am riding.

A warning horn blows but I do not turn. They will not catch me. All I need to worry about now is not getting shot on my approach to the castle. My choice was rash. But the other option was to let the stranger die. Well, not on my watch.

The sky begins to lighten as dawn approaches. I ride the remaining distance to town. My horses' hooves clatter on the cobblestones of the main street. As I ride through the square, I remember Ash.

I wonder what he will think when he realizes I escaped. He certainly was not up at the time that my new best friend and I made our debut in the courtyard. Ash would easily have been able to take us both down. The chaos of ill shot arrows would have been enough to have gotten off a good shot while we were distracted.

Things will be better this way, I think. He will not have to worry about keeping me alive, and I will not have to deal with the fact that he is the son of King Coriander.

My stranger groans and I turn to glance at him. "Just a few more minutes," I reassure him.

Then I turn my attention to getting into the castle without dying in the process.

Chapter 9

There are many side entrances to the castle, but I will not be able to reach them unnoticed. My guide is losing blood fast. I do not know how long he has, but the ride has taken its toll.

I can see the castle through the trees. I glance at my stranger. The skin around his eyes is pale. I enter the woods at a full gallop. The morning light sends the bright spring colors dancing on my green top.

My shirt is the perfect camouflage in my woods. I breathe in the fresh air. I have been away too long. When I left, it was still winter. Now, the spring flowers are starting to bloom and fresh growth lines the forest floor.

I pause at the edge of the trees. The battlements are swarming with soldiers. Currently, I am not grateful for our kingdom's record of having the best archers in all the surrounding areas.

I slide to the floor. Tying the bridle of my horse to a large oak. I drop my cloak and run.

A few things register as I fly through the trees. Soft pine needles under my feet. The song of a bird high overhead. The wind whipping through my hair.

I emerge at the edge of the treeline.

The archers see me, then a hundred arrows soar toward my chest. Finally, my training has some use.

I dive into a roll, arrows sticking into the ground where I just stood. I flip and slide, twirl and jump. Never staying in the same spot. Always moving.

I feel my mind giving into my body. Second nature and impulse take over. My feet slide over the dirt. Skipping. Barely touching the ground but to bound to my next spot in the air.

I left my weapons with the horses. There was no way I could take out all of the guards.

Anyway, half of them are my friends.

An arrow lands just to the left of my foot. How? I have been constantly moving. The shooter would either be able to see into the future, or be a horrible shot.

Or it could be him.

My eyes scan the battlements as I launch into another impressive set of sidesteps and flips.

There! In the center, slightly to the right. His favorite spot when firing on a target. Even in the archery range, my instructor never stood directly in front of the bullseye. But we moved past using stationary targets long ago.

They must be worried if they have him out. Mek never enters a fight without direct orders from my father. He is too valuable to lose.

Well, clearly I have their attention. Feet spinning in the dirt. Arms splayed out in bizarre motions. What can I do to show him who I am?

I slide to the ground, roll to the side. Immediately flip backwards. Sidestep. Flip again. Roll to the side. I sprint three steps. Slide diagonally. Up again. Back handspring with a half twist.

The ground beneath my feet begins to show a patchwork of letters.

I roll forward. Dance my way into a semicircle. Do a complex set of twists on the ground that lead me in another, slightly larger half circle. Spring back to the beginning of the original half circle. Back forward. Past the second semicircle.

My feet dancing across the dirt, I repeat the symbols I showed at the gate. The previously packed dirt displays my letters.

Dahlia.

An arrow slides between my raised arm and my ear. I feel blood trickling down my shoulder.

Hmm, I did not expect that.

The whiz of arrows continues to thunder around me, but I have eyes for one person. Only he is good enough to kill me. My feet continue moving, making use of my hands when necessary. But my eyes never leave his face.

Mek examines the letters. Then his eyes lock with mine. I left my cloak for a reason.

He considers me for a second, then raises his bow. He draws an arrow. Eyes still locked, he lets it fly, not to where my heart will be next, but up. The arrow soars into the sky, a perfect arc. I know where it will fall. I smile.

Mek always loved a challenge. Everything was a test with him. This is no different.

My feet spin in the arrow's direction. Leaping, I grab the arrow out of the sky, twist, and send it back. My throw lodges the arrow in the molding between the stonework on the wall a foot below Mek's chest.

Chapter 10

Time slows down. Arrows slip past me on all sides. But I am barely conscious of them.

My eyes never leave Mek's face.

For a second, I remember Ash. He knows that I am gone by now. Will I die at the hands of my friends instead of my enemies?

Ash's face swims in front of my eyes. His imaginary brown ones seem to meet mine. A smile flashes across his lips. Mischievous, clever, trusting. How could he be a Coriander?

For some reason, seeing him in my mind's eye reassures me. Still frolicking over the stretch of dirt in front of the castle, I raise an eyebrow.

Mek looks at the arrow, back at me, and nods.

"Hold your fire!" he bellows at the rest of the archers.

Puzzled, they turn to look at him. Officially, only an officer could give that command, but Mek carries prestige for his abilities.

The officer turns, too. Opens his mouth to protest, "Mek—"

"This one's friendly." Mek's commanding tone is as firm and as loud as ever. With the arrows gone, I pivot, bounding into the forest.

The stranger does not move. His dark clothes absorb the deep red blood that pours from the wound.

I fear he is dead.

My hand finds his wrist. His eyes flutter open. Deep brown. Alive.

Doubling over, I clutch my ribs briefly, gasping for air. Sitting alone for months has not been ideal fitness preparation, and my sprint dance has taken more out of me than I expected.

Taking one more shuddering gulp of fresh air, I straighten, grab the two bridles, and run toward the castle. The horses follow at a trot. As I reemerge, the heavy iron doors are just beginning to swing open.

All I can do is pray that this dear stranger has enough strength left to pull through.

***

I sit in the hallway. Anxious. My mother has been working on the stranger for more than an hour.

My parents are the best medics in our tiny kingdom. Not only because they have access to the newest remedies and herbal concoctions, but they also seem to know exactly what to do.

Few people have died at their hands and thousands have survived because of them.

They do not treat everyone. Only the elite and close friends. Other kings and queens come with their children to receive medical treatment.

They tried to teach me, years ago. A noble came in with a lung problem. My mother took me with her. She instructed me on the herbs to mix and the broths to stir.

The man kept coughing in a horrible fit. Finally, I couldn't stand it. I fled the room.

My mother finished her job. Later, she found me in the archery range shooting the catapulted clay ducks the trainer launched for me.

She tried to encourage me, but I refused to go back. The raspy cough, the blood on the handkerchief, the way his body contorted with each heave of air. I could never, ever deal with that.

Now, for the first time in my life, I wish I could stomach the blood, the moans, the pain. Wanting to help but not knowing how, my mother banished me to the hallway. Once there, I sat on a bench, hands clasped. Counting the minutes on the grandfather clock by the door.

After what feels like eternity, the door opens and my mother peaks her head out. I jump to my feet. Eyes alert. Scanning her face for signs of success or failure.

"Just his spleen. He'll live." Her voice is calm as always. Reasonable. Reassuring.

Mother disappears back into the room and my uncle emerges.

He hugged me shortly the moment I entered the wall, but immediately went with my mother to tend to the stranger. Now, he sits beside me, holding my hand.

I briefly wonder where my father is. Why hasn't he come to see me? No business can be more important. I satisfy myself with the fact that he is probably traveling to another kingdom, dismissing the factor that my mother should be by his side.

It makes sense that my uncle is here. He frequently rules in my father's stead when he goes out of the country. Sometimes, I feel sad for him. My father and uncle were twins. My father was born ten minutes earlier and that made him king. I push these recollections out of my head. I need details.

"How did you do it?" Out of all my questions, this is the one that bugs me the most.

That man knew the guard shifts like he was one of them. He knew every room. My guide somehow was just as good of a fighter as I was. His stealth, strength, and ability to read a situation were unique to someone with the best training.

"I don't know what you mean." My uncle looks genuinely puzzled.

"The man you sent to find me. How did he do it? He managed to avoid all the guards. The Corianders only tell each guard their own path, no one else's. Every guard is on their own schedule, yet he managed to lead me out. How?"

My uncle looks befuddled. "Dahlia, everyone we sent came back dead. We figured they had killed you by now. Our best spies were found by the border. Not one of them even made it inside the palace."

I frown, "Then who is he?"

"We were so busy cleaning the wound and stopping the blood that we did not take the time to remove his face covering."

Mother reappears at the doorway, "Chérie." Her pet name for me. I stand as she falls into my arms. "I thought we lost you."

"Who is he?" I stroke my mother's hair. I have never been the sentimental type.

"I don't know. Do you want to find out?"

I nod.

I still wear the outfit I left Tamar in. My sleeve is ripped from where the arrow tore it. I have wrapped a bandage around it.

My feet tread softly on the wooden floors. The stranger

lies on the table. His eyes are wide, nervous.

My mother and uncle stand at the foot of the bed as I cross to his side. I feel strangely nervous. I don't know why.

A complete stranger saved my life. How can I thank him? What will I say? Does knowing his identity make any difference?

As my hand reaches under his chin and pulls up the mask, I realize that knowing who saved me makes a big difference.

My mother shrieks. My uncle yells for guards, pulling my mother from the room. I stand by the table. Shocked beyond moving. Sure my eyes are deceiving me.

"Nice to see you too," Ash says.

Chapter 11

Guards swarm in through the doorway. Three forcefully escort me outside the room. My mother grabs me and holds on.

"He was the one who kidnapped you, wasn't he?" my uncle asks darkly.

I stand against the wall as the guards hustle Ash out of the room and force him toward the dungeon.

My conflicting emotions run their course through my body. First, shock. Seeing Ash and knowing he saved my life, committing treason in the process. Then, gratitude. He took an arrow in the back to reunite me with my family. After gratitude, confusion. The arrow was shot at me. It would have hit had I not turned my body.

Ash's body is dragged by. He catches my eye and holds it for a second before turning away. In that brief moment, I see the fear, but also that steady trust. The kind that says he will follow me wherever I lead because we are friends, no matter what.

Fourth, doubt. Ash could be trying to win my family's favor so that he could spy on my kingdom. Again, confusion. Ash could easily have come for diplomatic purposes, or he could have dressed up like he was in the village. No one would be any the wiser.

They are dragging him down the hall. I watch the slow trail of blood leak out from under the white bandage like a bottle of spilled ink on parchment. Blood that was so carefully contained by my mother before she knew who he was.

Sixth, embarrassment. I should have guessed that it was him. A mysterious man appearing in my room, equipped with a key and capable of traveling the palace corridors without running into the guard's uniquely scheduled paths. My guide had prepared horses for the journey and made sure the gate in the wall was open. Additionally, he had shot with skill that could rival my own. That in and of itself was suspicious.

A moan escapes his lips. Despite the pain medicine, Ash clearly feels every tug as they pull him along the ground, too weak to stand.

Finally, fear. Ash had shown up in the palace of his father's enemy, weakened and wounded. My father and uncle will prosecute him without a second thought.

Essentially, if I stay silent, my friend is dead.

These past few weeks I have gone back and forth between trying to trust Ash and hating him for what he put me through.

Now, for the first time since the village, I am sure that he is my friend. Like it or not, I have had enough time to get to know his actions, what he is willing to do, how far he will reach for his father. I know he will not use me as a pawn. Evil though his father may be, Ash does not use people to get what he wants. His heritage and his actions conflict in every situation that I have ever seen him in.

If he wanted to help me escape for his father's purposes, it would have been slightly too easy. Anyway, Ash would show that he was acting for his father. I know when he is acting and when he is real. Watching him in the village for a year has given me this knowledge. Ash would not use me as his father would wish. If he helped me escape, he did it for me, as my friend.

My mind travels to the dark, cold dungeon where Ash will be locked away. With the amount of blood Ash lost today, he will not survive the night. I am not going to lose my friend, not after everything else.

"Wait." My voice carries down to the guards at the end of the hall. What can I say or do to keep Ash out of that evil dank place? I look imploringly at my uncle. "He saved my life."

"He has many motivations for that. Mainly getting into the palace. He would have no way in without you." My uncle's stare is hard, sharp. I have never seen that look of hatred so intensely displayed in his features. "Take him away," he demands of the guards.

"No!" I find myself moving away from my family and toward Ash. I reach the end of the hall, effectively blocking their path, and kneel down beside Ash.

The guards are conflicted. On one hand, my uncle is currently acting as king and has the final say in everything. On the other hand, I have never spoken against my uncle in public and since I am friends with many of the guards, they trust me.

My uncle looks startled. He tries to read my face, but I wipe my features, staring back into those light brown eyes that usually hold such warmness and love but now show nothing but hate and the promise of death.

I take advantage of my uncle's silence. "Take him into the Juane Room. Set up a watch around the clock. Two soldiers at a time by the locked door. He will not be able to escape from there." My voice is stern and commanding, the orders coming out just as my father taught me to give them.

When the soldiers glance at my uncle, he stands stoic, impenetrable. Finally, he gives a curt nod.

Henry, one of my better friends in the royal guard force,

gives me a hand up. I realize I'm shaking. I slowly rise to my feet and walk behind the soldiers, watching the gold tassels on their boots swish from side to side as they march.

The guards deposit Ash on the bed. I sit on the edge of the chaise lounge. Henry glances at me, eyebrows raised. He is not allowed to question my decisions because of my rank, but it is obvious he does not feel comfortable leaving me locked in a room with only Ash.

I answer his questioning eyes with a reassuring nod and a smile. Ash is too weak to stand. There is no way that he will be able to overpower me, much less escape from a locked room with guards waiting on the other side. Anyway, after what Ash just did for me, I doubt he is going to try to kill me.

Henry accepts my decision to stay, nods, and turns to leave the room. As the door closes behind him and I hear the key turn in the lock, I rise from my position and walk to stand beside the bed.

I watch him for a moment, unsure of what to say. 'Thank you' seems lame after all he went through, but at the same time, what else is there to say?

Ash takes one of my hands in his large, warm ones. I smile down at him, glad that, for the moment, he is safe.

Ash seems to be struggling to stay awake, his eyes are heavy and bloodshot.

"He was going to… to execute you today," Ash whispers. Then, he rolls over and passes out on the soft yellow comforter.

My words of thanks die on my lips.

Chapter 12

"I still don't understand why you care about him, Dahlia." My uncle's voice is angry. "Yes, he helped you escape but you would have escaped eventually without him."

"I told you, he is my friend. He saved my life. Samuel was going to execute me today. We owe Ash our thanks." This is probably the fourth time I have stated this. Our conversation has been going in circles for hours.

I am tired, weak. I only received two hours of sleep last night and the adrenaline rush has stopped. I am worn out. But I need to win this fight. My uncle and I disagree on many subjects, but I am always respectful in public. Now, I have spoken against my uncle and for my father's 'enemy' in front of an entire battalion of soldiers. Wonderful.

"Grand Prince Ashton Coriander is going to be executed. There is no argument in that.

"His heritage is enough to kill him and that does not include the fact that he managed to brainwash my niece into believing he is her friend. Prince Ashton also kidnapped you and is the very reason you were tortured." My uncle, Prince Adkin, is very unhappy. This is the first time he has used the brainwashed argument though.

"Uncle, I knew him before I was taken." If my uncle can add new arguments, I shall add my own, "Ash had no idea I was a princess. Just like I did not know he was the Grand

Prince of Tamar."

My uncle looks shocked at this turn of events. "You knew him? How?"

"We met up in the village. I—" Before I have finished the sentence, I know I made a mistake. My uncle can twist the fact that Ash was in the village into a hundred different reasons for why Ash should die.

"Please," I beg him. "Ash is not King Samuel. He is different." I am running out of things to say. My brain seems dead and I am having trouble forming arguments, so I whisper, pleadingly, "Please, Uncle, he's my friend."

He seems torn. This is his chance to get back at Samuel for what he did to my mother, making my father pleased, yet his brother's daughter stands in the way.

My mother rises from the loveseat in the sitting room where we have been having this discussion. Crossing to my uncle, she places a hand on his arm. "Give the boy a chance, Adkin. He is not even of age."

She is one of the only people who can calm my uncle. He watches her for a moment, thinking. His broad shoulders are in the rigid posture that they always hold. His face contorts. Red lips opening and closing, weighing his decision carefully as he always does.

In this moment, he looks reminiscent of a mountain. Tall, weathered by winds for centuries, strong, yet he is still my uncle. In the hurricanes of life, he stands impenetrable, cold and hard like solid rock. But then spring comes, he smiles, the mountain comes alive with life. Birds and deer, trees and flowers, everyone wants to be around him, to share in the joy of life he emits.

My father and uncle are so similar and yet so different at

the same time. While my uncle is quick to punish, my father takes his time before declaring a verdict. Still, both are very serious when it comes to implementing their decrees.

I stand with bated breath. Ash's life hangs in the balance. I feel something more. A shift, a stirring. I fantasize about leaving my family to rescue Ash, just as he did for me.

For a moment, I see Ash, his lifeless form hanging from the gallows. The execution of a criminal. A commoner. I feel my heart tear in two. My throat seizes and I cannot speak. This fantasyland that my mind inhabits speaks of horrors I dare not dream of.

It was always my life hanging in the balance, knowing that every day could be the last.

That was hard. But knowing that Ash, a true, loyal, trustworthy friend, could be killed because he saved my life, that is unbearable.

I feel something else, a longing, a tugging in my chest. But I tell myself it will only be guilt that will hold me. Even as I think this, I know that if I let my uncle execute Ash, I will never leave this room, trying to figure out a way to convince my uncle to let that boy live.

In the future, I will become queen, be married, watch my children and my kingdom grow, but that will all be in the background. A hazy land that is too good to be true. Too shiny and bright to hold the world I deserve. For the forefront of my mind will fight, plead, beg, because I will never forgive myself if I let Ash die.

My eyes find my uncle's face. Imploring him to choose to let Ash live. I feel dependent, small. Waiting for someone else to make a decision for me.

"Fine, he can live. For now."

***

As I enter the Juane room, I notice Ash is wide awake and watching me. He sits up on the side of the bed and groans. His eyes squeeze closed for a moment as he gets his bearings. He looks pretty beat up.

His voice is horse as he speaks, "Now I know what it feels like to be you."

"Minus a bit of torture," I reply matter-of-factly.

"Yeah, well, I've got a feeling that's coming my way soon enough."

I move to the seat in the corner across from the bed and sit down. Sighing, I lean back in the chair. "You know my father and uncle really want you dead."

"Yeah, well, same here."

I groan. "What are we going to do?"

"Maybe try to stay alive?" he says with a shrug and a slight smirk.

That wasn't what I meant and yet that is exactly the problem. In his kingdom, I will be killed. In my kingdom, Ash will be dead in a few days after my uncle stops humoring me. Every other kingdom either has an alliance with my family or Ash's.

The crazy thing is that he is probably safest here, in my kingdom, where I have the most influence. My fingers twist my royal ring round and around my fourth finger on my right hand. It is a symbol of my status and the only one of its kind in the whole kingdom. It is my ring and is known by everyone in the entire kingdom. My mother forced me to change into royal clothes before my uncle berated me.

As I finger my ring, my mind searches for a solution.

When I am thinking, I always twist this ring. Round and round. When I first started going to royal meetings with my father, my mother forced me to remove all rings because I had rubbed every single one of my fingers raw.

I got better over the years, but I still twist it when I am thinking hard, nervous, or stressed. Normally a bit of each.

The question remains: what can I do to keep Ash alive? I cannot stay by his side at every minute. My uncle could wait until I was busy with some other business. No one would question the fact that my uncle executed Ash immediately.

The only reason I wasn't executed in the same manner was I had royal information. Also, it was probably because King Samuel wanted to dangle me in front of my father for a bit. He knew I was the most precious child my father had ever loved, and it would hurt him more to hear of my sufferings than to grieve and move on.

Round and round the ring goes. Ash seems to be thinking as well. His eyes fix intently on a spot on the rug. I peer at it too. Curious.

The rug is a beautiful pattern of golden vines creeping around the outside with light blue and pink flowers in the center. The vine has what would be flowers blossoming off of it, but the flowers form rings with precious gems inside it.

My mind goes back to the search. Twist, turn, round and round. The king and queen both have one similar to mine, but they are all unique. The inside of each ring is engraved with our names. With this one ring, anyone in Hazelton would accept a person and their motives without question.

Accept them without question!

My fingers fumble with the ring, "I have an idea!" I start stumbling over my words as I tug the ring off my finger and stand.

"If you ever need me, give this to the guards. They will return it to me immediately and I will come. This will also act as a deterrent to anyone who wants to kill you. This is a one-of-a-kind ring. Most people could get into anything with—"

"I know what the ring is, Dahlia. I've studied your kingdom for a long time. A while back, we even sent a few spies to try to steal one of them." Ash looks at me in an exasperated sort of way. "Let me tell you, your family keeps a good guard over those rings. You practically never take them off and when you do, they are under lock and key, as well as guarded round the clock. At one point, I knew every pattern of the rings' whereabouts. When you took them off, what events you wore them to, what path you traveled through the castle while wearing them. Everything. And still you managed to keep them away from us."

"That is what we were aiming for. Good to know that our policies work; they can be a pain sometimes," I say with a light laugh. I wait for Ash to say something, but he just sighs and gives me a small smile. Today has been taxing for both of us.

Taking his hand, I place the ring in his palm. "Keep it out of sight and only use it if you really need to." The severity in my voice sombers the moment. He nods, accepting the ring.

I realize the royal dinner is going to be served in ten minutes according to the clock in the corner. That is not something I should be late for. My mother is a stickler for manners.

It hits me that Ash has not had anything to eat or drink today. Shame hits me full on, flooding my cheeks red. I was so busy trying to make sure everything else was going to be okay that I totally forgot he needs to eat too.

"I'll have someone bring you dinner," I tell him. Then, I hurry out of the room.

Chapter 13

"You care about him." My mother rises from the window seat. Clearly, she has been waiting for me in my bedroom.

After the confrontation with my uncle, I had crashed onto my pillows and passed out.

Now, she requires an explanation.

"He cares enough about me to help me live." My sentence comes out as more of a sigh than a claim. "I owe him my life."

"You do realize you also owe him hours of torture, chérie."

I flinch. "That was King Samuel's specialty."

Her lips purse at his name. "Seeing that he is King Samuel's son, I would advise you as your mother to steer clear of him and as your Queen, I would demand more caution."

This conversation is making me uncomfortable. My mother is suggesting there is more between us than the truth.

I change topics.

"So, where is Dad?" I ask her, "I haven't heard anyone mention him since I got back. Is he on a trip or something?"

She stares at me, completely caught off guard. "No one told you?"

"Told me what?"

"Dahlia," My mother's voice is gentle. Her tone carries the same softness she used to tell me my pet rabbit, Fanny, died. My heart drops to the pit of my stomach, the smile sliding off my face. "Your father's really sick. I didn't realize you didn't know."

My nerves calm slightly. Sick isn't dead. He'll heal. But why does my mother look like she's already lost him?

"Can I see him?" I ask, wondering why I wasn't taken to him immediately last night.

"He's extremely ill. The doctor isn't allowing anyone to see him. He worries your father's disease might be contagious." She pauses for a moment before adding, "Dahlia, he also said if we gave your father any sort of illness, even a mild cough, it would be the end for him."

"So I can't see him?"

"No." My mother shakes her head sadly. "Your uncle and the doctor are the only ones let in and out of that room. Dahlia, the doctor even refused me sending a maid in to clean up."

It seems uncharacteristic of my father to not allow my mother to enter when she is the person he cherishes most in this entire world. My father and uncle are not always on good terms, so I wonder why he gives my uncle preference over my mother.

I study my mother's face. Her cheeks are shallower than usual, and she appears pale. At first, I had attributed it to my absence. Now I see my father's sickness has taken a larger toll on her than I ever could.

"I send him notes every day, though. Your uncle goes to see him to discuss business and ruling the kingdom. He always tells me your father's reply. Apparently, he has grown too sick to write." My mother's face whitens with the last sentence.

"Why is Uncle Adkin allowed in there if Father could be contagious? Also, isn't the doctor worried about Uncle getting Father sick?"

"No, Adkin wears a face covering and is very careful. The

doctor was hesitant about letting him in, but he insisted. Your uncle would not be separated from his brother. He claimed to be unable to rule and make important decisions without him."

My mother seems to have accepted the fact that she isn't allowed to see her husband. Yet, her tone delivers bitter feelings to my ears, clearly unhappy that my father will see my uncle but not her.

"Will he live?" I am months away from my eighteenth birthday and being old enough to rule Hazelton, but that does not mean I feel in any way prepared for the task. I had been counting on my father's continued reign for quite some time.

My mother only shrugs and pulls me to her. I let her wrap her arms around my shoulders. I feel cold. Empty. Isolated on a turbulent sea and my raft has just been punctured, leaving large holes in the frail wood. I doubt it will hold me for much longer.

Moving away from my mother, I sink onto the edge of my bed. "How long has he been sick?"

"A week after you were kidnapped, he started showing symptoms." My mother drops onto the plush comforter beside me. "At first, we assumed he was just worried about you. When he got sicker and sicker, I sent for the doctor. I couldn't find anything wrong with him. The doctor suggested confinement for your father. He believed your father was unfit to rule, so I transferred power to your uncle."

I watch her face. The way she said *uncle* wasn't as friendly as it normally was.

"He's made some changes around here. I wish I had waited longer. I could have given some to you." She clearly looked distressed.

"What does it matter?" I ask, "You can give them to me now."

"No, I can't," she replies. "Now, either your father must get better or we must wait until your eighteenth birthday. Otherwise, your uncle has full control."

She stares out the window. Lost in thought. I wonder what my uncle has done that could make her want to rid him of power. She answers the question before I ask it.

"My brother-in-law tends to follow King Samuel's policies more than your father's and mine," she says slowly. "I fear he will begin to restrict women's abilities to make decisions without their husband's approval."

I freeze. My uncle? Restrict women? He had always been the most progressive of us all.

What had changed him in the time I was gone?

My mother rises and heads for the door. As she places her hand on the knob, she turns to look over her shoulder. "Another thing you should know: he sent Mek to kill you yesterday."

She hesitates, as if wanting to say more but then turns the knob and exits the room. I'm caught by the way she emphasized the *you* in her statement. Almost as if she suspected him of knowing it was me.

With this morbid thought, I watch her close the door, leaving me in gloom.

Why would my uncle want me dead? Sure, he could rule the kingdom if my father had no heir, but I had always been my uncle's favorite. What had changed?

Did he actually want me dead? Was I making things up? My mother never said that he knew but it was implied. I felt her hesitation again. The look in her eyes that cautioned me from asking what she could not answer. Because if that answer was true, it would be treason to voice.

I replay my welcome committee. My mother had rushed

to help Ash after giving me a quick peck on the cheek. My uncle had not acknowledged me. I assumed he was trying to care for Ash. Now, I find it strange he did not even try to talk to me until after the stranger had been taken care of.

***

I stand to the right of my father's throne as a nobleman confronts my uncle about the fact that a peasant cut down a tree that was, as he claimed, two inches on his side of the property line. The tree was cut to make a crib for the infant that was about to be born.

The nobleman demanded reparations. Honestly, this trivial stuff kills me. I want to tell the nobleman to go pick on someone else of his own stature but know it is not my place.

Finally, my uncle tells the nobleman to bugger off. Only he does not say that. He politely reminds the nobleman of how blessed he is with riches and land. Then he points out that the nobleman owns his own small forest. After giving the nobleman some perspective from his life to the life of the peasant, my uncle commands the nobleman to pay the peasant double his salary this week in preparation for the baby.

The nobleman leaves, grumbling about the fact that royalty always side with the poor.

I turn as a guard enters the throne room. My uncle immediately looks more alert. This piques my interest.

"Leave us," my uncle commands me.

But why? My father allows me to know all the royal secrets. I want to protest but know it is not my place. I worry the conversation involves Ash.

Last night, I had a maid bring him dinner and some water. The bedroom has a built-in bathroom and shower, so most likely he was able to wash up.

My uncle has not confronted me about him again. I have enjoyed the peace and being able to catch up with my family. At the same time, I feel like I am stepping on pins and needles. Knowing my uncle is looking for any piece of information to convict Ash forces me to watch my words.

I am uneasy. Ever since my conversation with my mother, I have been suspicious of my uncle's actions. He has given me nothing to work with. Despite my ceaseless attention, I notice nothing out of the ordinary. Maybe my mother meant nothing by her comment and I'm trying to fill in blanks that aren't even there?

As I leave the throne room, I make my way down to the archery range. I have not been able to catch up with Mek yet.

The range appears empty as I enter. I grab a few spears and throw them into a few targets, hitting the exact center every time. I hear footsteps outside in the corridor and freeze. I am back in that dreadful place. I hear King Samuel's guards coming for me.

I shiver, my arm lifting the spear, poised to throw. My head tilts slightly, listening to the sound of their feet. Walking down the hall, soft footsteps that sound light as snow, coming to take me to Samuel, so he can watch me scream.

Not today, I tell myself. Today, I am going to fight. My jaw hardens and I tense. My eyes focus on the door. The footsteps stop. One guard. They will never even see me coming. My breathing is shallow, deadly quiet.

I see the knob turn, almost in slow motion. My arm begins to move forward, the spear just barely in my grasp.

The door opens and Mek steps through. My brain stops. Mek is not in Samuel's palace.

He is back home with my parents. I cannot comprehend

what is happening.

My hand releases the spear. I know, without looking, it will find his heart. Finally, my brain reconciles where I am. Mek is in my home, and so am I. My eyes widen in alarm. My mouth opens to yell for him to move, duck, do anything to avoid the spear.

Mek sees me. His eyes register the spear, and he falls backward, landing on his hands in a sort of bridge. The spear skims his chest as he dives back, passes over him. By that point, he has already used his momentum to flip his legs over his head, following the spear's path.

The cry is caught in my throat. My brain is reeling, and I feel like I am going to pass out.

Thus, I can only stand and watch as Mek launches himself toward me, tackles me to the ground, and puts a knife to my throat.

I am caught off guard. Mek slams my head into the ground, and I lose consciousness.

***

I come to, confused and disoriented. There seem to be a thousand tiny men with pickaxes trying to hack their way into my brain. Mek is sitting in the corner, watching me.

A soft moan escapes my lips as I sit up. I wait for the world that is spinning before my eyes to right itself. When the floor finally stops moving, I turn my head slightly to focus on Mek. Even the slightest of movements makes me feel like someone is setting off fireworks in my brain.

"Are you normal now?" Mek asks bluntly. "Because I can knock you out again if you're not."

That is one of the reasons I love Mek. He gets right to the

point, no beating around the bush, no fancy language; he is not one to waste words.

"I feel fine. The world is the one with problems. It keeps tilting." My head can't seem to keep the world straight.

"It'll stop in a day or two."

"That's encouraging," I say dryly.

Mek watches me for a few moments. Finally, he just asks, "Who did you think I was?"

I hang my head. If there is one person in this entire castle I trust wholeheartedly, it is Mek. And I just nearly killed him. Thankfully, he is also the deadliest person in this kingdom, so he was able to avoid near death.

Somehow, he is always on the alert and, though he has thoroughly encouraged me to do the same, I always get too comfortable and relax.

"I..." My voice falters and I give another attempt, "I... I thought you were one of Samuel's guards. I thought... I thought you were coming to get me."

Mek's face remains neutral, but his eyes harden, just for a second. If he had not taught me how to hide my emotions himself, I would never have noticed it.

"Next time, let's try a stealth attack. That way you can work on sneaking up on someone. Throwing a spear is too easy and then you are defenseless." Quick and brusk, he gives this command as if we had merely been practicing my fighting methods.

I notice the white bandage he has wrapped around his torso. His shirt was sliced right down the middle and there is blood seeping through the clean fabric.

"Mek, your chest..." I falter again. What am I supposed to say? That I didn't mean to hurt him? I was aiming to kill him. Anyone else would be dead.

"It was a good throw," he tells me sincerely. "Just make sure the person does not use the door to shield themselves."

I feel sick. Mek should not be reassuring me. I should be punished. I am a danger to everyone. If I lose myself again, someone might die. Somehow, though I am careful to hide my emotions from my face, Mek knows what is going on in my mind. He always does.

"You can keep yourself in control. I trust you." His voice is genuine and his golden eyes hold mine. So intense, they see everything. "Let's work on taking down a target without killing them. We might want them for questioning."

We spend the next four hours working on different techniques for sneaking up on someone, disarming them, and beating them in hand-to-hand combat. I fight some of the other guards and heavyweights my father employs. Then we move on to the swordsmen and archers.

I fight Mek a few times. I never win. Though I can beat everyone else, he somehow knows where I am going before I even make my move. I am slowly getting better. I have even gotten in a few good blows and once I managed to trip him. When I tripped him, I was so shocked I had managed to actually do it that I stopped; that split second was enough for him to tackle me from the ground. The fight was over, but I still felt elated.

Mek beat me handedly ten times in a row after that before letting me go.

"Just don't get a big head and you might beat me someday," he told me as I walked out the door.

Chapter 14

The world does stop spinning after two days. Just like Mek told me it would.

Unfortunately, the headache persists. My uncle has stopped calling me into the throne room to try to give royal advice. Thus, I have been spending more and more time with Ash.

Some days, I take all my meals besides dinner with him. He is funny and talkative. I tell him about what is happening outside the castle walls. We debate about how to best handle issues. Whether we agree or disagree on the method, both ideas are normally superb and would work either way.

Ash is a wiz at building things. I gave him a few short pieces of rope, some small slabs of wood, and a nail to create holes in the wood. He created a swing and hung it from the ceiling.

On one hand, my uncle will be furious that the architecture is vandalized. On the other, Ash created a working swing set. Seeing that I have never been allowed to play on them with the other children, I love going into the Juane room.

For some reason, none of the soldiers or maids have said a word about it to my uncle. I am grateful to them for that and wonder if their silence is due to respect for me.

It has been two weeks since I returned home. Ash's wound is healing. He can walk around and exercise slightly without breaking it open again.

Knowing that my uncle would never permit Ash to leave the Juane room except to be led to the dungeons or the gallows, I did not bother asking his permission when I told the guards that Ash and I were going for a walk.

They refused to let us go alone so I stationed twenty around the perimeter of the gardens. I hate being watched but my desire to spend time with Ash wins out.

We spend the day together. Eating a picnic, picking flowers, walking. I let him try to braid my long dark hair with flowers. He actually does a decent job so I leave it in.

We watch the sunset, and I have a gardener fetch some painting supplies from the castle. Neither of us is a skilled artist but we do our best to imitate the bright patterns displayed across the sky.

Once evening has truly begun and the sun has set, we go inside. Ash returns to his room, escorted by twenty guards, and I quickly tie my braid into an intricate bun before heading to dinner.

I enter the room with a smile on my face, still reliving the happy time Ash and I had spent. My uncle is sitting at the head of the table, my mother at the foot.

Good, we are all here. I'm starving. I move to take a seat in the middle but one look at my uncle's face tells me that dinner is not coming anytime soon. The smile drops from my face and I slide silently into my seat, eyes on the tablecloth. Slowly, I lift them to his irate face.

"Dahlia, when were you planning to tell me that you were taking our most valued prisoner outside of the castle walls?" His voice is even, barely containing the fury burning in his eyes. I wish I had kept staring at the tablecloth. If I couldn't see his eyes, I might have believed he was only mildly bothered.

"He needed the fresh air. We had fun." I can tell this isn't helping. "I practiced my painting skills," I say hopefully. I can't help it, my eyes scan the tablecloth, as if it will somehow provide the answers to make my uncle like Ash.

He barely whispers the next sentence, but it carries across the room. "Never again. Ever. Every time you enter that room, you must have direct permission from me."

My shock and outrage give me the strength to raise my eyes from the table.

"I would not question me," he states. "I will kill him, now or in a year. The Corianders are nothing but evil. You should not be spending time with a bad influence. I don't want you to get hurt but you keep putting yourself in harm's way. You give me no choice."

I want to protest, cry out against the injustice of it. Despite my anger, I hold my tongue. I know my outburst will only encourage my uncle to hurt Ash.

I study the tablecloth for the rest of dinner. My mother and uncle make meaningless small talk. Who wore what to someone's party. How lovely my mother's hair looks tonight. When the next royal meeting is going to be. Just as we are finishing dessert, my uncle makes one last comment.

"I announced the ball today."

My mother looks exasperated as she mouths 'really?', piquing my curiosity. I glance at my uncle. I have not heard about a ball. Normally, I am the one to plan them. My father hates figuring out the logistics of balls and my uncle always avoids them if he can.

My uncle does look sheepish as he looks back and forth

between my mother and me. "I forgot to tell you. We are having the ball for you to meet suitors from other kingdoms. Your mother and father think it is time for you to get married."

Clearly, he omits any opinion he has on the matter. I assume he wanted this announcement to come with a bit more explanation, probably some compliments, and a loving hug. Not after a fight. I know he means well, but I cannot stand it. It just seems all wrong.

I leave the table without saying a word.

Chapter 15

The next few days are a flurry of action. What colors will the drapes be? What music to play? Should we have more chocolate delicacies or vanilla? Does violet appear too imposing and royal? Should the cake have spikes or flowers?

Every single decision is weighed against everything else. Making sure we have the perfect look and give off the best impression possible. During one of the preparation days, my mother finds me sitting at the window, watching the clouds come and go.

As she gently lowers herself down onto the window seat beside me, I continue to watch the sky. The birds are out and about. Free from any care and any worry. Able to go where they please and do what they wish.

My mother's arms encircle me and I break down.

"I don't want to get married," I whisper in a child's voice.

I know I'll have to. I need to pass on my lineage and da-da-da-da-da. Still, everything about it seems amiss. And there's another reason that I'm not sure how to explain to myself, much less tell it to my family. I feel like I am betraying Ash.

There's nothing between us. We are friends, that's all. But a part of me wonders, if I opened that door, would he walk through it? We care about each other deeply, that much is obvious. But a small part of me wonders if Ash cares about more than friendship.

I try to push the thoughts from my head, telling myself that we certainly get along well and we are productive when we work together.

I realize my mother is watching me. I must have zoned out.

"Chérie, you don't necessarily have to marry any of the men you meet at the ball," she says. "We just decided it was time to start the process of looking for someone."

She plants a kiss on my head and turns to go, but then adds one last comment, "Your uncle won't admit it, but I think part of this is because he is worried you will get too attached to the Prince."

With that said, she immediately turns and calls to a maid down the hall, "Jane, dear, I love the way you have arranged the colors, but those wall hangings need to be higher so that people can enter their rooms." She squeezes my arm and walks off to continue her work.

Staring out the window, I think of my father. I worry about him. For me to meet suitors without his approval and encouragement seems daunting to say the least. How will I know if they are good?

I need his seal of approval.

With that in mind, I mentally write my letter, asking him all the things I could never voice in person for fear of my uncle reading the letter as he delivered it to my father.

I stay by the window, watching the sky and the birds until I cannot ignore my duties any longer. I make my way to the kitchen where I sample dozens of chocolate delicacies, deciding which would make the cut.

I pick out the frosting colors for the numerous miniature cakes that will adorn the towering stone carvings of sea creatures: the theme for this ball. Creating mixtures of blues and greens that peak in waves for the dolphin statues on blueberry cakes. Bright pink, orange, and yellow sea flowers with bits of green seaweed for the turtles on vanilla. Vibrant coral mixed with sea succulents for the seals on red velvet. Dark chocolate swirled with pure vanilla in an inky mixture for the octopuses on chocolate cakes. Golden sunlight shining through the water for the starfish on lemon cakes.

I only have one cake left and I decide to make a special addition. Though my mother has already chosen the specific sizes and flavors for all the cakes, I feel that, if this ball truly is for me, I should be able to spice it up a bit.

I tell the cook to do the clam ones specially. I want perfect balls about two inches wide on the end of sticks that sit inside the clams. Every one of them shall be dipped in chocolate icing but the similarities stop there. Exquisite interior flavors that burst in the mouth will bring a surprise to every bite. Banana, cheesecake, coconut, orange, coffee, chocolate with cherries, rainbow, cinnamon, strawberry, apple crumble, caramel, and raspberry are but a few of the flavors that I select from a long list.

Satisfied with my decisions, I make my way up to the ballroom, where I help my mother direct the servants on where to place certain decorations.

In the late afternoon, I am fitted for a new gown. My mother refuses to tell me what it will look like, and the seamstress has her lips sealed, taking my measurements and leaving without saying any more than "lift your arms," "hold still now," and "chin up a bit."

Exhausted, I make my way to bed in a trance. I have not seen Ash since my uncle demanded his permission. Every time

I have asked, he has found some chore for me to complete.

I have been extra efficient, finishing all of my work as well as some of my mother's and uncle's. The ball is still two nights away and I have completed almost everything.

The next morning, I find my uncle sitting at his desk.

Before I can say a word, he asks, "Have you finished decorating the ballroom? Also, have you picked out the decorations for the cakes?"

I nod.

"The gardeners might need some assistance in knowing which plants to pull and how to prune some of the bushes."

"I instructed them last night," I tell him.

"What about your outfit? Is everything completed with that?"

I reply in the affirmative.

My uncle rubs his eyes. He sounds tired as he says, "You really want to see him?"

"Yes."

He nods. "Only for an hour. I want you to do some training with Mek."

I nod quickly, hurrying from the room. It's not a lot of time but at this point, I am grateful for any. He still managed to give me something else to do but in no way is it a chore. Normally, I would treat training with Mek as a break.

The guards allow me to enter the Juane room without question. Ash raises his eyes from the book he is reading and smiles, but I can see the worry etched in his features.

I get right to the point. "My uncle didn't like how much time we were spending together, so he forbade me from seeing you without his direct permission."

Ash just watches me, knowing me too well to believe that

this is what bothers me so much.

"He is also having a ball tomorrow night in the hopes of finding me a husband."

Ash nods his head, closing the book and placing it neatly on the side table. "At least you get a choice."

His response surprises me. I expected him to sympathize with me. To rant about how unfair the whole situation is. Instead, he has taken a defeated yet hopeful position.

I glare at him, waiting for an explanation to this pitiful response.

"My father has been planning to have a ball for all of the rich, beautiful, prominent women in three years. In his plan, he intends to watch how graceful they are. Then, he will pick my wife from the lot, and we will be married within the next week. You might have limited options, but you still get to make the final decision."

Somehow, this makes me feel slightly better about how my parents are going about the process.

"I'm so sorry," is all I manage to say.

"It's okay. I'm used to it. I have been raised to get married and be the king after all."

We continue to express our sympathies for each other and to point out the bright spots in the situation for both of us. The hour passes quickly and soon it is time to say goodbye.

I stand to leave, and he rises as well. Surprised, I find myself taking two steps forward and throwing my arms around his neck. I bury my face in his jacket and his arms encircle me, holding me tight like he is afraid that if he lets go, I will never come back. We stand like this for a moment and then break apart, looking sheepishly at each other.

"That was… nice," he finally says.

"Yes," I agree awkwardly. "It was."

I smile. Then I exit the room, wondering what I was thinking when I agreed with him. I am about to go to a ball to find a husband, yet here I am expressing physical affection for the only person I will never be allowed to marry. I feel like kicking myself for even doing it but a small part of me whispers that it was nice, just for a moment, to have those strong arms around me, to feel safe from the world, protected, cared for.

I really need to stop thinking about Ash. There is only one place where that is an option. I go down to Mek and throw some sharp objects around to keep my mind from overthinking it. It was just a hug, that's all. I keep telling myself this as I shoot arrows, throw spears and daggers, fight with a sword, and wrestle.

Chapter 16

I wake up in the morning to see my maids hovering over me. As they bathe, powder, and polish me, they chatter about nonsense; I tune them out. I watch my hair drip water and see the gleam from the light reflecting off my nails. They are blue waves with foam. Twisting, twirling, and leaping.

Finally, after hours of prep, the dressmaker shows up with my dress and unfurls it. I can't help myself. I gape. My mother has designed yet another gown that would make any man fall in love with me. No need for curtseys and etiquette, just show them the dress and there will be a line of them proposing around the block.

"Mom," I gasp. "It's beautiful."

Beautiful is not a good enough word for it. The skirt billows down like a crashing wave, peaks gleaming with sunlight. The top is slim fitting with long sleeves that give the impression of raindrops falling when I move. The back has slits in it that open and close when I move, like waves on sand.

Then there are the pearls, thousands upon thousands of pearls. Around my neck, hanging from my ears, in my hair, swirling like sea foam down my dress. Every color, shape, and size.

It radiates power, strength, and might, but there are the soft touches that show gentleness and love hiding underneath.

I feel like the ocean, strong and powerful. Able to kill thousands and yet willing to gently float someone on their back and carry them away. I can be a strong current or a gentle tide.

Thunderous crashing waves or little ones lapping at your toes.

My mother helps put the finishing touches on the dress before going to finish getting ready herself. Surprisingly, the dress does not weigh barely anything. I imagine I am floating as I make my way toward the entrance to the ballroom where I am to make my debut.

I perceive the doors are opening, watch my mother and uncle move out into the glamorous crowd, and follow with precise steps. The silence that drops when I enter hits me like an arrow in my stomach. You can hear every tinkle of the pearls as I move through the doorway. No one moves.

The announcer ends his speech and men rush forward to greet me, compliment me on my looks, kiss my hand. Eventually, I have met every single one of them. Slowly, I move into the crowd.

The ball looks amazing. The billowing curtains and sea creatures make me feel as if I am swimming in another world. Men wear everything from pirate's garb to sea captain's tailored suits to octopus tentacles.

While some of the outfits appear truly bizarre, most enhance the looks of the wearer. A man in a scaly fish suit asks me to dance but I refuse. I informed my uncle yesterday that he was to be my first dance.

I spot him making his way through the crowd toward me. Detaching myself from the jumble of suitors tottering around me, I make my way toward him.

Taking my hand, he bows low and kisses it.

"May I have this dance?" he asks clearly and politely.

"It would be an honor," I respond sweetly.

I did not want to have to choose which suitor to dance with first. I figured if I had my first dance with my uncle, then I could dance with anyone and not worry about having to pick a good first dance.

We waltz around the floor by ourselves and slowly other couples join in. There are many other eligible girls here who are looking for a partner themselves. After I dance with my uncle, I dance the foxtrot with an oarsman, the cha cha with a drunk salmon, the tango with a pirate who steps on my toes, and the salsa with a chicken. Honestly, *only* every single invitation specifically stated we were having a sea themed party.

The deserts are a huge hit. A drunkard openly proposes to me on the dance floor. I calmly decline the invitation and signal for the guards who drag him out of the room. I meet a nice pufferfish until he starts rambling on about how beautiful our children will be.

There was an eel who caught my attention for a few moments but during our second dance I realize he keeps glancing at an octopus girl in the corner.

The whale brings me a drink and some chocolates but the moment he takes off his mask to eat his chocolate, I know he is not for me. The wrinkles of a man three times my age sag around his eyes and the bloated cheeks are enough for me to wonder if he stores the chocolate in his mouth to swallow later. I politely excuse myself and head back to the dance floor.

My mother comes over to check in and see if there is anyone I like. The look of disappointment on her face when I tell her no cuts me to the heart. I promise myself to try harder.

I spend some time with a seahorse, but the man wheezes constantly and can barely rasp out a sentence. From him, I move to a walrus who seemingly has never met a woman in his life. He keeps talking about how amazing it is to be dancing with me and how beautiful I am and how this can't actually be happening that I dump him at the delicacies and move on.

A shark catches my attention by speaking in beautiful poetry the whole time until I realize he is speaking about himself. I detach myself and wander around the ballroom until I see a young man who has arrived late to the party. He stands off to the side, looking unsure of what to do.

Unlike the majority of the men, this one does not have a mask on. He wears a slim fitting white captain suit. He actually looks like he could be a sea captain with his tanned skin, strong arms, and cocky smile.

I approach, standing near him to see if he is bold enough to ask me for a dance. He does. After introductions, we twirl around on the floor for a while and make light conversation. Seth avoids all of my questions about where he is from and what his occupation is.

Meanwhile, he asks many questions himself. Seth is funny in a self-deprecating sort of way. When the conversation turns to ball themes, he says once he considered having a ball with himself as the theme, but then he realized everyone would dress up like him and none of the ladies would come.

People slowly begin to leave the ball. As the numbers trickle down, we continue dancing, eating, and talking. We have much in common.

Eventually, we are the only ones left besides the band. I offer for him to stay the night in the palace, but he declines.

"I enjoy long carriage rides," Seth tells me. "May I see you again?"

"It's up to you," I say. "If you decide to come back, I can't stop you."

"Then I guess I'll have to come back."

Seth smiles and I smile back. I tell him I will walk him to the front door. For the first time since the ball was announced, I feel hopeful. It wasn't a bad idea to have the ball after all.

As we walk, chatting and laughing, a guard peeks around the corner, then quickly ducks back. A few seconds later, he neatly struts around the corner, making his way toward us. It seems like curious behavior, but I am at ease in my own home.

He draws closer to us, and I am about to let it slide when I see the shift in his gait. The slight tremor in his hands. The sweat on his brow. Right as he steps past me, he turns, drawing the dagger that was concealed in the folds of his uniform. I hit the ground, grabbing Seth by the hair and yanking him along with me.

I use my vantage point on the ground to spin the man's legs out from under him.

Overpowering him easily, I twist the knife from his grasp, pulling his white leather glove with it and getting a glimpse of the tattoo on his wrist. Clearly, he is highly trained, for with a simple twist, he frees himself from the ground and disappears down the hall toward the front door.

Scooping up the knife, I am about to follow him when I see that Seth, who I violently moved out of the way, was cut. The long gash along his arm has already left a pool of blood on the ground.

He sobs like a child, holding his arm in a pathetic manner and not even trying to stop the flow. He clearly has no idea how to protect himself or others. I rise to my feet, smooth the wrinkles out of my dress, and turn to speak with the guards who are rushing down the hall.

Chapter 17

After having his arm cleaned, sewn up, and bandaged by my mother, Seth informs me that we have the worst security system he has ever seen. He also tells me a woman should never fight a man, whether they have a knife or not.

"You should have let me handle it," Seth states irritably. "If you hadn't acted so rashly, I wouldn't have been hurt."

"No, you would not be hurt. You would be dead," I try to explain. "He drew his knife and tried to kill us. If I had waited, we would be dead."

My voice rises hysterically as I push my crumpled hair out of my eyes. How on earth does he think he could have handled that better? I had to pull him to the ground! Then, he simply laid there and cried like a baby. Now he wants to pretend he is the strong manly one while I was the damsel in distress?

I know I should hold my tongue, but I allow the words to spill anyway. "You couldn't beat a toddler in a fight, and I'm supposed to let you handle it?" My voice is harsh. "Seth, you are a pitiful wimp of a man. If you want to pretend you're anything else, the only person you'll fool is yourself."

I know I've overstepped a boundary. His brow creases and his jawline hardens. "Fine. Be that way," he snaps, stalking out to his carriage.

I should go after him, but my proud self holds me back. It was mean to call him pitiful, but he earned the title. Anyway,

I almost never back down when I know I'm right. Even if it might hurt the other person.

I am heading back into the castle when a curious fact hits me. The guard that attacked us was in our castle's uniform. But, his tattoo was the symbol all Tamar servants wear. The only way someone from Tamar could enter this castle would be in uniform and those uniforms are stored in the castle. No one from Tamar is allowed in the castle.

I stop in my tracks.

Spinning on my heel, I march down the hall toward Ash's room. One of the guards opens his mouth to stop me but a good look at my face shuts him up. I don't even care right now. I feel betrayed, hurt, used.

The doors swing open, and I stomp through. The guards immediately shut them, probably scared they will get brought into the fight.

Here I am spending my time trying to keep Ash safe and alive, feeling that I owe him my life while he steals from me and sends people to kill me. So much for... well, whatever there was between us, because it's gone.

Ash sits up in bed, sees my face, and quickly slides out the other side, placing the bed and side table between us. I slam the knife from the assassin into the canary wood table. Ash takes one look at it and pales.

"Dahlia, let me explain..." His voice cautions but I'm not in the mood for listening.

"You sent an assassin to kill me. You obtained a castle uniform. I don't know how but I can't believe I trusted you. I fought to keep you alive, and you tried to kill me." I am screaming but I don't care. "I had faith in you and gave you my friendship. And look where it got me. My uncle was right.

You and your father are just alike. He tried to warn me, but I didn't listen. You fooled me once, but never again!"

"Dahlia!" Ash sounds thoroughly hurt, which makes no sense. I know he is good at falsifying his motives but if he is trying to act, this is a terrible way to go.

"You are an evil person. To think I cared about you even the tiniest bit makes me sick." I don't understand why, but with every word I utter, my heart seems to break into even smaller pieces. Part of me wishes he would fight back. Yell and scream. Give me a reason. Instead, he just looks sad.

"Dahlia, please." Ash looks defeated, small.

"Don't pretend you didn't know. You sent him to kill me. He had your symbol from your kingdom."

"Please let me explain," Ash pleads. "Dahlia…"

I glare at him for a good moment before nodding. Despite my anger, I want there to be a reasonable explanation. A solution that does not end with Ash's head on a platter. Because this is exactly what my uncle wanted. He has everything he needs to convict Ash and no one who will stand in his way.

"I did not send Blaze to kill you." He sighs and rubs his eyes. I keep staring daggers at him.

"It's a long story." When I don't stop staring, he slides into the armchair and continues, "Do you remember the day we met?"

Well, that is a long time. I give a curt nod.

"There was a fight at the bakery. An unidentified young man attacked a guard and claimed to be the rightful king of Hazelton. He then fled the bakery and was never seen again. Or so everyone thought." He pauses for breath. "As you know, all of the guards travel in pairs. While one guard went to get a danish from the bakery and was attacked, the other guard waited outside the store. That guard was quietly abducted. He was new and nobody noticed. Blaze changed into the guard's uniform and replaced him."

I am still angry, but my rage is slowing. At least Ash did not officially steal from my family.

He did not even know me while the plot was taking place. Still, he could have told me that we had a spy in the palace. My sense of betrayal and rage surge back to the surface. I am also deeply concerned about the safety of our palace staff. The screening system must be improved.

"Blaze infiltrated the palace and gained information. He was the reason we were able to find your carriage." Ash winces as he realizes he probably said too much. "He was not meant to kill you, only to gain information. My father must have given him new orders once you escaped."

It would not surprise me if King Samuel had given the spy new orders. Yet, somehow, this spy, Blaze, infiltrated our place, stole our information, and was the reason I was tortured. But what of his accomplice? Ash seemed to not wish to touch on that topic.

Ash quiets his voice, "You're wondering what happened to the original man who started to fight."

It still amazes me that he knows my thoughts so well. Ugg, I'm supposed to be mad, but he is so hard to find frustrating.

"As the accomplice was escaping home from the village bakery, he saw a beautiful young woman. Disobeying orders, he spoke to her. He continued to come to visit her even though he knew it was dangerous. If he was caught, he would be killed."

I don't know how this relates to me being nearly killed but I have to admit it is interesting.

"The young woman was charming. She found delight in the simplest things. Another reason the boy kept coming back was because the woman was mysterious. He could not find any information about her." Ash has still not broken eye contact. He pauses for a moment and then says quietly, "The boy was me and the girl was you. I'm so sorry, Dahlia. By the time I knew who you were, it was too late. I could not speak about Blaze without giving him a death sentence. I didn't realize he would actually try to hurt you."

Ash genuinely seems sorry, but I am still struggling with the first part. How could I have missed the fact that he actually started the fight? My brain feels fuzzy. I sink into the armchair across from Ash. I want to be angry with Ash, but my heart is just grateful he did not give the kill order.

Ash turns his gaze toward the table. "They finally have a reason to kill me." He nods to himself.

"No." I surprise myself with the fierceness in my voice. "No, I was the only one who saw the tattoo. There aren't any more, are there?"

Ash shakes his head, "No, we wanted to test it out first. The only person we sent in that I knew about was Blaze."

"Good. Then he was a random rebel working for his own intentions. There is nothing else that can link you two together."

Slowly, Ash rises from his chair, as if in pain. He moves to the side table and pulls out the knife. I had it in there pretty deep, but Ash frees it with a simple tug. Walking back toward me, he holds out the knife in his palm.

Ash grimaces, "Dahlia, take a closer look at this knife."

I see it then. Engraved into the steel, the symbols of Tamar. I know if anyone in the entire kingdom sees this knife, they will easily be able to convict Ash. My brain wakes up.

Searching for a solution.

After this attempt on my life, I will not be able to leave the castle by myself. The guards will see the knife in any way that I attempt to dispose of it.

I could try to sneak the knife into the stash that Ash and I used to leave Tamar. I would need to get around the guards then too.

If I kept it, I don't know what would happen if my family found it. Then, where in the castle could I hide it? Servants clean every day. Fluffing cushions. Dusting behind armchairs. Mopping floors.

There seems to be only one solution to this mess. I must get the knife out of the castle. Doing so would involve another person. I would have to get someone to help me. Most people would be willing to help but the moment they saw the knife, they would back away or worse report me.

Racking my brain for an answer, I tap my fingers on the arm of the chair. They come away dirty. Odd.

"Do they not clean your room?" I inquire of Ash. I had not noticed that no servants entered or exited the room. I suppose it would be dangerous. Theoretically, Ash could take one of them hostage.

"No," he replies.

Now that I think about it, I don't believe they cleaned my room in Tamar.

But that is beside the point. I do not trust anyone to help me take the knife out of the palace and there are others I do not wish to get involved in this matter. That leaves me with one option.

The knife must stay where it is. I turn to Ash just as he seems to reach the same conclusion. He withdraws the knife from where he was holding it in front of me and slides it into the back of his pants, pulling his jacket over it so that it is not visible.

If Ash is found with the knife, the soldiers will kill him before trying to get the knife off of him. Another part of me worries about giving Ash the knife in the first place. I trust him not to hurt me, but he may use the knife to try to escape.

"Please don't kill anyone with it," I tell him.

I won't hold it against him if he uses it to escape; I would have. I would just prefer not to have any of my friends killed in the process.

"I'm not going anywhere," Ash reassures me.

"You can escape. I'll help you if you want."

"Where would I go? I committed treason in my kingdom. Every other kingdom is either allied with your father or mine. Both would have me killed."

It's a valid point.

"Well, if you change your mind or want someplace to go, let me know. I'll help work it out." I feel sad. Ash has no home to return to because of me. Guilt threatens to close my throat but I fight it.

The clock strikes four in the morning and I realize how late it is. I rise from the armchair and head toward the door. Ash opens the door for me and I step through. One of the guards raises an eyebrow at me but I scowl at him and move on down the hall.

My uncle is standing by my doorway, buzzing with questions. I realize I spent two hours in Ash's room. My uncle was obviously worried but I feel like the questions are reaching me from far away.

    As wave after wave of exhaustion hits me, the plush cushions on my bed look so inviting. I mumble something about telling him everything in the morning and close the door. I climb into bed with my dress on and welcome sleep.

Chapter 18

My mother gives my maids the day off and wakes me herself at noon. She does not seem distressed by the crumpled dress. Her tone and manner are all gentleness. I dress in a skirt and slim fitting top while she picks out my jewelry.

She talks only of the ball and the fun outfits. Skimming over the parts where I was attacked and disappeared into Ash's room for two hours.

We have lunch outside in the gardens. The summer sun has not become unbearable just yet. The servants bring picnic baskets filled with bread, cheese, and a whole roast turkey, presliced of course. There are jams, jellies, and delicacies of every kind ranging from chocolate cakes to little puff balls of blown sugar.

It is delicious.

My mother, never one to pry, simply sidles around the topic that is on both of our minds until I finally break.

"Please just go ahead and ask. The suspense of what you want to know is killing me."

My mother takes a moment to fold her napkin before speaking, "Why did you go to Prince Ashton? Was he responsible?"

I take a deep breath, collect my nerves, and answer blankly, "No, Ash had no hand in that man trying to kill me." That much is the truth. Ash didn't even know about the assassination order.

"Then why did you go to him? Do you have proof otherwise or just his word to contradict it?"

Gosh, my mother knows me so well. Carefully displaying my features as calm and nonchalant, I quietly say, "I just wanted to make sure. I know the Corianders have a kill order for me so I wondered if someone had infiltrated the palace. I know it is unlikely for the palace to be breached, but since we had the ball, I just wanted to be sure."

I really only answered the first question, but my mother does not question me. She knows I am weighing my words and not telling her everything.

"Well, I am glad the Corianders had nothing to do with that. It would be worrisome to know they had managed to get a spy into the palace." Her words are calm but her eyes are intensely locked with mine.

So she knows, or has at least guessed who the assassin was. I look away. Maybe not the most tactical move but she knows she is right by my silence.

"There is no immediate threat from Ash," I say.

My mother nods her head. "I know, chérie."

I look at her questioningly. What is that supposed to mean? Is something happening to him?

"You would tell us if he was a danger," she says, "Your father and I are more important to you than he is. You would not let him hurt us."

Her voice is calm. She trusts me, and with good reason. I am the most family loyal person ever. Even in conflict, I still love them. Even if I don't like them.

But my heart tugs in Ash's direction. During this time, he has become part of my family. I care about him. I stop myself from going down that path.

Turning my attention back to my mother, I ask what plans

we have for the rest of the week. She launches into her spiel about dinners and councils, meetings and permits, documents and signatures. Apparently, there are many unhappy nobles, but then again, there's always a list.

My mother loves planning and excels at it. I know she will go on for quite a while and I try to appear attentive while letting my thoughts wander.

The roses in the garden smell sweet and their dainty colors range from bright red to soft baby blue with every other color in between. I am mentally compiling a new bouquet of flowers for my room when something from a passing gardener's conversation catches my attention.

"…And we still need those flowers for the two balls next week…" The older gardener instructs the younger one, "…Cut from those bushes there and that one there…"

They meander away but my thoughts are spinning. Two balls? Three in the span of two weeks? What are my parents thinking? Are they so desperate for me to get married?

I had turned to hear the gardeners better and when I turn back, my mother is watching me in silence. I jump right into my question, now is as good a time as any, I guess.

"Why are we having two balls in the coming week?"

My mother purses her lips as she considers her answer.

"Your father and I wish for you to meet all the eligible suitors from the surrounding kingdoms. Then you can pick your favorites to receive follow up invitations to more events."

I glare at her, "How many events do we have planned?"

"Enough for you to find a husband, however many it requires."

The notion that they didn't say anything about having more than one ball planned, all the suitors, and me picking my favorites ticks me off.

"Well, you are clearly not letting me meet all the suitors or letting me pick my favorites since you blatantly left at least one major suitor out."

As soon as the words leave my mouth, I want to retract them. My mother's face pales. "So you do consider him a suitor, and a prominent one at that?"

My silence says more than I ever could. My mother knows me too well. Even if I protested, she would see right through it.

"Dahlia, just remember whose family he comes from. I don't want you to make the same mistakes I did."

I nod. Since we are on the topic, I go ahead and ask, "Why can't Ash come to the ball? He is as much of a suitor as any of the other men."

My mother looks pained as she says, "He can go, but be careful, he's still a Coriander."

I grin at my mother, not able to help myself. Thanking her profusely, I am giddy. I pepper her with questions about the details of the next ball.

When is it? What is the theme? How many people? Where are they from?

My mother answers all my questions. Pleased to see I am excited for the ball. I can't wait to tell Ash. It will be so nice to have a confidant at the ball. I know I need to wait though so I channel my excitement into the conversation about the ball. My mother appears pleased with my interest in the ball, and I don't say anything to dissuade her of that.

Eventually, we move into the palace because the heat from the sun is scorching. The gardeners are hauling water to keep the flowers from wilting and the newly painted statues glisten in the sun. I go to train with Mek.

I practice jujitsu with Mek. We have been working on it

for over a week now and he is no longer going easy on me. After successfully ending a fight by doing the bow and arrow choke on Mek, he releases me from training.

A servant gives me a note summoning me to my father's office. I follow instructions and knock before entering.

I love my father's study. As a little girl, I would spend hours reading through the books on the floor to ceiling bookshelves that cover every wall and even go above the doorway.

Of course, there are many hidden doorways in the bookshelves with book levers to activate them. I read every single book on his shelves to make sure I knew where the doorways were.

I even helped install a new one with a safe room behind it. Hopefully never to be used but it had to be designed by just our family to keep my father safe in case we had a traitor.

My uncle sits behind the desk, smiling. I walk in and sit in front of him.

He watches me for a moment before speaking, "I heard that you convinced your mother to allow Prince Ashton to go to the next ball."

My heart drops into the pit of my stomach. My uncle is still smiling which is disconcerting. "I figured that if I had to meet all suitors, I might as well invite every single one of them."

I'm not sure why my uncle looks so happy. He hates Ash. He should be furious, yet he is absolutely beaming.

I feel unease creep into the bottom of my stomach.

"Anyway," my uncle says nonchalantly. "To the point. Dahlia, your cakes were such a hit last time that I would love for you to design the ones for this ball too. The theme, as you know, is black and white."

I smile. My uncle knows how much I love decorating and designing food. "It would be my pleasure."

I curtsy and leave the room. I am excited for the ball, much more so than the last one.

But my uncle's smile still irks me. It was a happy smile, yet he clearly knew something I didn't.

I grab my sketchbook and design a few desserts. After giving the details to the kitchen, I go to dinner. As I enter the foyer, I hear my mother and uncle arguing.

My mother's voice is condoning, "—won't forgive you. They clearly care about each other."

"Exactly, that is why it will work." My uncle, stubborn as ever, pushes his point, whatever it is.

"I'd like to still have a relationship with her after all this. There are other ways to work this out."

My uncle's voice is still firm. "I'm…"

My foot steps on a creaky floorboard. I wonder who they are talking about. They clearly don't want me to know because when I open the door, they are talking about how excited they are for the ball and all the details that accompany it.

They normally tell me things. I wonder who they aren't getting along with and what they are planning. Who does my mother care about? Why is my uncle willing to lose a relationship with someone? They must be important to my family if they are arguing about the pros and cons of breaking ties.

I didn't catch enough of the conversation for it to make sense. It bothers me that my mother and uncle aren't telling me everything.

Chapter 19

Ash shakes his head at me as I explain how I convinced my mother to let me invite him to the ball. I don't understand why he isn't happy about it. I have gained him freedom from his cell of a suite and gotten him a ticket to a ball.

"Why aren't you excited?" I finally ask him.

"Dahlia, what do you think will happen when one of the suitors notices me, Grand Prince Ashton Coriander, at the ball?" Ash asks. "If they are friends of your parents, they will surely be confused and angry at your family for allowing me to come. They might even break ties with your family because of it. That would be the least of my worries. Every single one of those suitors is skilled in martial arts. They may decide they will take care of me for your family and present my dead body to your parents as a gift. Would you be excited about that?"

I give a little shake of my head, biting my lip. My happy bubble has popped, and stark reality returned. "Now, let's present the other option: the suitor is from a kingdom that is in the middle or is allied with my father. They will know I committed treason and am to be brought in dead or alive to Tamar. Whether they decide to kill me there or to drag me to my father, either way it does not end well. My father will prosecute me. Personally, I'm not too excited about that option either."

I'm at a loss for words. Somehow, I was blind to the endless negative possibilities. Ash's concern forces me back to the actual danger he is in, but I'm not about to give up on him going to the ball.

"The ball is themed black and white," I state hopefully. "You could easily have a mask. No one would know it was you. We could fit your suit so your body looks different too if that helps."

Ash is not convinced.

I cannot believe my mother finally allowed me to give Ash a bit of freedom just so he could turn it down. I will not settle for no as an answer.

"Ash, we could pull it off. I have the seamstress coming tomorrow to measure me and I'll just have her pop in and measure you while she's at it."

"And you trust this seamstress with the fact that you are keeping the Grand Prince of Tamar in the palace without prosecuting him? I have a feeling word about my whereabouts will spread fairly quickly after that visit."

I sigh exaggeratedly. "I'll have one of the maids measure you and give the seamstress your measurements."

I smile hopefully at him. Ash can't seem to find a complaint with my suggestion, so he nods slowly. My smile turns into a grin.

"Great! I'll send her in sometime later today."

Ash looks less than thrilled but I got my way. I smile and bid him adieu.

Henry meets me outside the door and with a small wave of his hand sends the other guards down the hall.

"Everything okay?" I ask.

Henry glances down the hall and at all the doors around us. This is a guest wing, but no one is allowed in the rooms on this hall because of Ash.

"Shall I escort you to your evening walk?" Henry asks

nervously.

I don't have an evening walk. I can't stand walking pointlessly in circles around the garden all by myself. It drives me nuts. Henry knows this.

"That would be very kind of you, Sir Henry," I say formally with a slight curtsey.

We walk in silence to the garden and out into the wood grove. There is a little gardener's cottage that is hidden by the trees. Henry pulls me behind it.

Now I'm sincerely worried. Why is Henry going to all this effort to talk to me in private? Is everything okay? What is going on that he feels cannot be even discussed inside on an empty wing?

"Are you sure about inviting Prince Ashton to the ball?"

Henry's question throws me off guard. First, because I'm still trying to convince myself that Ash is safe around all the other suitors. Second, Henry could be fired for that question.

I glance around at the woods. Now, I understand why he dragged me outside and into the grove. No one questions the royal family. Ever.

"What do you mean, am I sure?" I'm whispering now too.

The staff does what we say. The town may talk to some extent behind closed doors and in the alley ways but no one ever openly questions royalty, much less to their face.

"I mean, do you really trust him that much?"

Looking Henry straight in the eyes, I answer firmly, "Yes."

With anyone else, this conversation would be out of the question. I should never let someone question me, but Henry is my favorite, and he normally has good suggestions when I ask for them. He has never tried to give me advice on his own.

Henry bites his lip, glances at the woods again, and says,

"Why?"

I raise an eyebrow. He grimaces. I have never been questioned this way by anyone besides my parents.

And maybe Mek on occasion but only because he was questioning a move I made, not anything other than work related.

I squint at him, trying to make up my mind about what to say.

"Well, for starters, he saved my life and brought me home. He had plenty of time to kill me if he wanted to." I stop to collect my thoughts. I'm tempted to add that Ash was my friend before I was kidnapped but it would be foolish to disclose that information.

"Henry, I trust Ash because he is my friend, and he hasn't given me a reason not to. There's not much more to say."

Henry glances around again and then asks, "What if he isn't supposed to kill you? His father didn't. Maybe his mission is to kill your father or your mother. King Samuel still wants to kidnap the Queen and I know he hates your father with a passion. Ashton could be using the ball to get close enough to your family."

Henry's remarks make sense, but I refuse to let them change my mind. I trust Ash, right?

I seem to be the only person able to see who he is. Is everyone else just not giving him a chance or is my vision clouded?

"Ash would never hurt my parents. Anyway, they have guards to prevent that. Every suitor at that ball is going to be a potential threat." I brush away the concerns but underneath I am worried.

Henry made a good point and I have no way to judge

Ash's methods. "Are you willing to just risk your parents' lives like that?"

Henry knows he's pushed his luck too far as soon as the words leave his mouth. He opens his mouth to apologize or take his words back, but I cut him off.

"Ash is coming. Don't question me again." My words come out commanding, sharp, and angry. Henry has no right to question me about the precautions I am making for my parents' safety.

I spin on my heel, marching into the palace and away from Henry.

A tiny voice inside my head tells me Henry has a valid point, but I tell it to shut up.

I remember how happy I was that Ash is allowed to come to the ball, put a smile on my face, and avoid Henry for the rest of the evening.

Chapter 20

Today is the big day! A flurry of maids enter and exit my room in rapid succession. They powder makeup on my face, dress me in swirls of black, and pull up my hair with black diamonds.

The dress is gorgeous. I love my seamstress.

Walking to the doors leading to the staircase which spirals down to the dance floor, my black heels clink on the hardwood floors.

Glancing through the doors, I catch a glimpse of all the suitors milling around. My mother and uncle glide up behind me.

"One finishing touch," my mother whispers in my ear as she wraps a blood red shawl around my shoulders.

I have to admit it; it is a nice touch. The red makes me stand out and contrasts beautifully with the complete black that covers me from head to toe.

The doors swing open and I descend. My mother and uncle follow a few moments later, settling into the ornate thrones where they will watch the dancing from on the balcony.

One by one, each suitor approaches and bows, kissing my hand. Some have overdone their costumes by styling their hair in white powder or painting their skin with swirls of black and white that mix to form gray.

One gentleman has on a tux made out of white ostrich feathers and eggshells. I have to admit that the idea was there, but the smell is almost unbearable. I am grateful for my long black gloves.

Every gentleman that approaches has some form of face covering but none of their voices match Ash's. I begin to worry something has happened.

The numbers of gentlemen begin to dwindle as the line becomes shorter and shorter. The angst I feel in my stomach grows with each passing man. My cheeks hurt from smiling so much and I feel like a puppet bobbing up and down over and over again.

Finally, the last gentleman approaches. I want to cross my fingers as I pray a small prayer.

The man is covered from head to toe in black powder with glittering white jewels covering his black coat and white undershirt. He bows and kisses my hand. As he rises, I look into his eyes but, instead of the dark brown I hope to see, they are sky blue: beautiful but not what I want.

Disappointment and worry tumble around in my stomach like a bull fight. I see Henry standing in the back of the ball room. Our eyes meet and he mouths, "You sure?"

I raise a dangerous eyebrow. I don't know where Ash is. My stomach feels like it just got thrown in the mixer. And Henry continually questioning my motives is making me furious.

As I glare at Henry, he turns to the guard by the door and nods. The doors swing open, and another gentleman enters.

The man wears no makeup or powder on his skin. Dressed from head to toe in white with a pure white mask covering his eyes and nose. The suit is gorgeous, and the lack of makeup and extra design distinguishes him from every other suitor in the room.

Bowing low, he approaches and kisses my hand, just like every gentleman behind him, but when his eyes rise to meet mine, they are deep brown and steady.

My smile widens.

"This may not be customary and forgive me if I am too forward, but may I have the first dance, milady?"

I chuckle. The host of the party gets to choose their first dance. Ash knows he is going out of order. I must ask and he must accept not vice versa, but I decide to go with it.

"That depends, my dear sir, on whether you plan on disbanding all rules and traditions or only some very boring ones."

"Oh, only the boring ones, princess. I like the exciting ones."

I smile, "I would love to have my first dance with you."

The band begins a tune and Ash leads me out onto the dance floor.

One hand placed firmly on my back, the other gently holding my hand, Ash guides me around the floor with smooth even steps. I'm surprised by how good he is at dancing. I figured he would know how to dance but he never misses a beat. He must have had an excellent teacher growing up.

"Dahlia." My eyes meet Ash's as he takes a breath. "It may be improper of me to say this, but you look absolutely gorgeous tonight."

I can feel my cheeks flair red with a blush as I reply, "Thank you, my seamstress did an excellent job, didn't she?"

"She did but I wasn't talking about the dress." He takes another deep breath, looks me in the eye, and says, "I was talking about you."

My heart flutters with his words like butterflies trying to escape. You could make toast on my cheeks. But my feet don't miss a beat, continuing to glide right along beside Ash.

I'm unsure of what to say. Ash's comment has opened a floodgate of emotions I've been hiding from myself.

"I overstepped a line, didn't I?" Ash says as I fumble with my brain to try to create a response. "I'm sorry. I hoped you would feel the same way."

His hands loosen but I grip his tighter with mine.

"I do." I hurry to reply, worried he might let go altogether. "I just couldn't find words to express what I felt."

Ash smiles and I feel warmth spread from my cheeks all the way down to my stomach.

His hand tightens in mine as the song ends.

"I'm supposed to go dance with everyone else," I tell Ash.

"Personally, I would categorize that as a boring tradition."

I laugh. "It is a boring tradition, but I still must follow it for the moment."

Ash sighs. "I will see you soon for another dance."

"I would expect no less."

Ash squeezes my hand and I turn to face the swirling mass of gentlemen surging forward to request a dance.

The night goes by in a blur. I dance with every gentleman, make small talk, and keep an eye on where Ash is.

I cannot think straight. I feel like I am flying. Ash is such a close friend of mine. I hadn't realized I was hiding so many feelings inside me. Now, I know I've loved Ash this whole time. It feels so good to know he feels the same way.

I crane my neck around the gentleman I'm dancing with to catch a glimpse of Ash. Our eyes meet and he smiles. The gentleman goes to spin me. My eyes are locked on Ash's and the man runs right into me. We both stumble backwards away from each other. I see Ash laughing from across the ballroom, but can't catch his eye. I need to pay attention so I don't mess up again.

Eventually, we get another dance.

As Ash dips me, I see Henry moving toward us. I straighten and turn to meet him.

"The queen and interim king request your presence on the balcony," Henry says with a bow. "The gentleman is not welcome."

I purse my lips. "Thank you, Sir Henry."

I turn to Ash, "I'll be back for the next dance if you are interested."

"It would be an honor."

I follow Henry up the stairs and into the balcony set aside for the king and queen. Curtsying low, I rise to see my uncle turn to a guard and say, "Wait a moment."

"How are you enjoying the ball, chérie?" my mother asks.

"I love it! The colors were an excellent idea, and everyone is so nice." I leave out the fact that Ash has confessed his feelings for me.

"Wonderful! I see that you have been able to dance with everyone," my uncle chimes in.

"Yes, they are all… well mostly excellent dancers."

My uncle is smiling and at ease but my mother's smile looks forced.

"We have something that needs to be done and that requires your acting skills," my uncle says.

My mother purses her lips and remains silent.

"What can I do to help?" I want to get back to dancing with Ash and my uncle is talking so slowly and carefully. It is royally annoying!

"We need to see who is really devoted to you, so we devised a plan. In just a few moments, a swarm of 'unknown' men, who are really our own soldiers, will sweep into this very balcony and manage to kidnap you. We need to see which men will go after you. Our thinking was that the ones who made it to you would be potential suitors."

The plan sounds devious but not terrible yet. I am not sure why my mother looks so unsupportive.

"So what's the catch?" I ask.

Again, my mother remains silent, which is extremely uncharacteristic of her.

"Ah," my uncle says, "I missed a part of the plan. Those who make it to you *alive* are potential suitors. The ones who are killed, well, they clearly aren't strong enough to make a suitable king."

My face pales. "You can't kill these men. If they ever found out you were behind it, you would have…" I meant to go into how there would be wars and the kingdoms would break alliances. There are no suitors who do not come from a prominent allied kingdom besides one.

It hits me as I trail off that my uncle does not intend to kill any of the other suitors. If need be, they are collateral damage, but he only intends to kill one person. Someone we both know will go after me without hesitation. Ash.

"No," I tell him. "You can't possibly be trying to do what I think you are." I am scared. My uncle has never been like this.

I shake my head again and again. "I will have no part in this."

"You can go willingly or not. Opting out isn't an option." My uncle meets my determination with his own.

"No," I say again. "I am opting out."

My uncle glares at me for a second before turning to my mother and saying, "I gave her a chance, didn't I?"

Being referenced to as if I am not even there is hurtful to say the least. I open my mouth to complain when my uncle motions to the guard by the door to the balcony. I watch as the door swings open and soldiers dressed in black swarm in.

Chapter 21

My training immediately kicks in. I am fighting for my life but there are so many of them that it is overpowering. Henry, who was waiting by the door, jumps into the room and begins to fight alongside me.

My uncle tells Henry to stand down but instead of obeying like he always has, Henry grunts, "Never."

My heart warms to having a friend who will fight beside me, but a man dressed in black takes a chair and slams it down onto Henry's head, knocking him out cold. There are so many men surrounding me that I can do nothing as they drag Henry out of the room. My uncle draws the curtains to the balcony.

I focus on the men, taking out one after another. The music is so loud that all the dancers have no idea what is going on upstairs. I take down three more men and do a handspring into two more.

As the curtains close completely, I glimpse Ash sprinting around the edge of the ballroom, eyes trained on our balcony. Leave it to Ash to be the one person who spots the problem.

I try to yell for him not to come after me, but my voice is muffled by the curtains and drowned by the music. I doubt he heard me and even if he did, would that stop him?

My effort to communicate with Ash places me in a poor position and before I know it, a bag has been placed over my head and I am bound and dragged out of the room. My mouth is gagged.

All I want to do is scream for Ash not to follow me. They will certainly kill him if he does. I want to curse these guards and my uncle. Finally, Ash and I were open about our feelings and now I've lost him again.

At some point, I feel my feet give out under me as the world fades to black.

***

I wake in a cold cell. The air is cool and clear, signaling I am on a mountain. My uncle's betrayal burns deep in my chest as I climb shakily to my feet and walk to the bars of my cell.

I was correct. From the bars extends a short flat slab of stone, a small wall, and then open air with the horizon in the distance. Where are we?

My castle can only see mountains in the far distance. How long was I out? How far did we travel?

My rage burns slowly in the bottom of my stomach, as a cauldron grows to a boil, threatening to overflow. I push against the bars, but they do not give. Frustrated, I begin kicking them. A guard rounds the corner and I realize the platform leads to stairs on both sides.

"Stop it," he grunts.

I gasp in indignation. How dare he! I am royalty and though I do not recognize him, every person in my kingdom knows my face.

His comment startles me so much that I actually stop kicking the bars. He commences to turn and trudge back up the stairs he came from.

I silently begin to examine the bars. There are no locks or key holes to be picked. As my fingers trace the outside of one of the bars, something bumpy interrupts the smooth metal.

My thumb and forefinger trace the outline. It feels like a combination lock, but it is built right into the metal bar. I have never seen something like this before.

I slide my whole wrist through two bars and twist it to see if I can get a better grasp of what I'm working with since I cannot see it.

I go to bend my wrist backwards to mess with this strange lock, but the metal stops my wrist.

"Ouch," I can't keep from whispering.

It is truly painful. My wrist is at such an odd angle that the metal has caught it. I try to pull it back inside to no avail. Finally, with great difficulty, I yank my wrist back into the correct position and slide it back through the bars, rubbing it ruefully and staring out at the horizon.

Part of me wants to curl up and fall back asleep. My head is throbbing, but I know I have to keep going. Ash is out there somewhere, and my uncle has plans to kill him. Ash won't stop till he finds me, so neither will I.

I shove my wrist back through the bars and keep working.

After a few hours, I hear footsteps on the stairs. I slide my wrist back inside and scoot to the back of the cave. A different guard, younger and less experienced, bounces up the steps.

He glances at me before continuing up.

A few moments later, the older guard who has no respect for royalty stomps down the stairs.

A shift change. I am being guarded by multiple people and there are most likely more guards stationed below.

Huddled in the back corner, I begin to think. I know the older guard could hear the bars being kicked from where he was stationed. The other guards most likely couldn't.

Otherwise, they would have come too.

The new guard is less experienced and more likely to make mistakes than the older guard. He also is my best chance of getting someone on my side because he doesn't know about the kicking yet.

I doubt he would just let me out, but I need to get out of this cell and find Ash. To do that, I must prey on the inexperience of my guard.

I go back to the gate, slide my wrist through, and twist it, though not enough to get fully stuck. I am flexible enough that it looks bad.

Instead of letting myself only a tiny grunt of pain, this time I exaggerate. "AAAHHH," I scream. "Oh my! Oh my! Ouch! Ouch! Ouch!"

I hear footsteps and keep up my complaining until the young guard rounds the corner.

He takes one look at my wrist and pales. Clearly not meant for gore, I wonder how he managed to even get into the army.

Catching his eye, I put on my pleading, in pain, face. "Please," I moan. "Please help me fix my arm."

He hesitates.

"It hurts."

Again, the young guard contemplates me.

"Do you promise not to try to escape if I help you?"

"How could I with my arm like this?"

It kills me to make promises I cannot keep but I promised myself I would protect Ash and I take the liberty of lumping this into that category.

"Anyway," I tell him, "it's not like I could overpower you."

Easily, I think inside my head. But the young guard only

knows normal women who have not been trained in the martial arts.

My arm is starting to cramp from the awkward position and the lack of blood flow. I make my face into the young, innocent girl I was taught to display.

"Fine," the young guard says seriously. "But if you try to escape or ever tell anyone about this, I'll stab you through the heart."

The severity in his voice cracks me up and it is all I can do to display my afraid face to complement his threat. I am tempted to burst out laughing for the stupidity. He just told me what his first move would be. Now, I know he will reach for his sword when I escape.

Poor boy, I think. He will suffer from this mistake.

Walking up to the gate, he turns the numbers and symbols on the mechanical lock.

Then, from around his neck, he takes out a key, places it in one of the symbols on the mechanical lock, and turns the key. The bars begin to swing outward.

Keeping my arm in position, I walk with the door. My back is to the young guard when I feel his blade on my neck.

"One wrong move and you're dead."

I remain still and silent. He seems satisfied with my compliance and sheaths his sword. I can hear Mek screaming 'MISTAKE!' and telling me to start over.

The young guard approaches. I listen to his footsteps on the stone. Take deep breaths. Wrenching my arm free, I turn, tackle him to the ground, pin his body underneath mine, and yank the chain from around his neck.

I stand and as he clambers to his feet, I kick him back into the cell and swing the door shut. It locks with a clank.

He never even had time to reach for his sword. I memorize

the mechanical combination and then mess up the lock.

Slipping the key around my neck, I move to the staircase and peek around the corner.

There are no guards in sight.

The young guard who is now in my cell starts yelling at the top of his lungs. I walk back to the cell. "Will you shut up?"

The young man marches up to the bars screaming insults at me. He goes to draw his sword and I punch him in the temple, knocking him out. He falls backward, hitting his head on the stone. He is still alive but the few brain cells he might have possessed have most likely fled.

"Thank you."

I glance up and down the stairs again, but no one is coming. I now see that the stairs circle out of sight. Is this a tower?

I figure I have a better chance of escaping if I go down than up. I make a left and begin my descent.

My heel clinks on a pebble and I glance down to see I am still wearing the black dress. The red shawl was lost somewhere along the way. I slip off the heels and continue on bare feet, making no noise.

As I round a corner, I begin to hear men yelling. They sound like they are taunting someone.

I continue my descent until I see the edge of another cave come into sight. My first instinct is to try to pass without anyone noticing. If they are focused on something else, it should be easy to pass the opening. The sky is beginning to look like dusk.

I wonder if I was out for one day or two.

The men cheer again, and I move to the edge of the cave

and peek around. They are all circled around a man tied to a chair.

I move my head out of sight and take a deep breath.

Something seems off as I peak around the corner again. The man seems familiar. I vaguely wonder if I know him when I hear the man cry out.

The sound makes my blood run cold.

I forget about Ash, my family, escaping. All I can think about is my friend, strapped to that chair, being beaten because I couldn't protect him.

All I can think about is Henry.

Hearing the men cheer makes me snap. I swing around the corner, taking down two unsuspecting guards with my high heels. The third takes a knee to the crotch and another knee to the head.

Backflipping over one of the men running toward me, I land behind him and draw his sword. Kicking him into two other men, I disarm four more soldiers.

Once all the soldiers are easily disarmed and knocked out, I free Henry from the chair he was tied to. He appears to be all right besides some bruises on his arms and face.

"You okay?" I ask him.

"Yes," he groans as he rises. "Thank you."

I nod, glancing around for a place to put the knocked-out soldiers sprawled around us.

They will wake up soon.

There are only two bars in this cave, one on either side of the entrance to the cave. They look like they are there more for style than anything else. I yank on one of them. It holds steady.

"Let's hook them to these," I tell Henry.

It takes almost half an hour but eventually we get all the

men handcuffed around the two poles and take all their keys.

"This way," I tell Henry as I make my way back toward the stairs and downward. He catches my arm, turning me so I look right into his eyes. "Thank you."

I nod. "Of course."

I twist my arm slightly and he lets me go. It bugs me that he felt comfortable grabbing my arm, even if it was to thank me.

Taking the stairs with a slow jog, I don't even notice the guard as he rounds the corner. I am so preoccupied with my thoughts about how to tell Henry kindly that he has pushed my boundaries multiple times in the last couple of days.

I almost bump into the guard before I realize he has gone to draw his sword.

Tripping him back down the stairs, he lays still at the landing below.

Henry and I are almost around the next curve when I spin around and dart back up to the guard. I slip off his jacket and hand it to Henry. He slides it on. The jacket is a little big, but it helps disguise him slightly.

As we move down the stairs, we take out guard after guard. As a team, we do not function well. Henry seems to feel he has something to prove or maybe he is still smarting from the fact that he was overpowered, but every guard he encounters, he nearly kills.

His gusto to take on a guard before I have a chance surprises me. He knows I am far more skilled, yet he darts ahead again and again.

Multiple times I have to catch a soldier by the coat or jacket as Henry flings them over the railing.

After the tenth soldier is nearly tossed to his death, I cry out in exasperation, "We're not trying to kill anyone."

Henry looks a little sheepish and lets me take on the next few guards we encounter on the stairs.

Just when I think these stairs will go on forever, the steps open up onto the top of a hill. I can see trees below us. They aren't anything like the forests in our kingdom. Some are tall, gnarled, and truly ancient. They sprout golden fruits from among their tiny white blossoms. Strange trees that appear as old as time itself.

Others are not from our kingdom, but I've seen them in picture books. I can see some ash trees with their light-green, oval shaped leaves. One looks like a fir tree, but it might be a pine for all I know.

I take off at a jog toward the forest. I do not like being so out in the open. Henry follows without question. The sun is almost set and the mountain behind us is lit with the most extraordinary colors.

Glancing around, I do not see a soul. It is eerily quiet. Upon entering the woods, I spot a regular footpath that probably leads to a town or cabin where the men live.

Another trail is hardly worn and branches off into multiple directions once it leaves the meadow. I pick one and hurry along it. I do not need to run into any more soldiers today.

How I got here, I don't know. The main path could hardly have room for a horse and the one I picked is barely visible to the naked eye.

Mek's training proving useful once more, I make my way around the base of the hill just inside the tree line. Henry follows just behind me but makes so much noise that I have to stop and ask him to take off his shoes. That makes it a little better.

We circle the entire mountain but find no other trails. The main road, if it can be called a road, appears our only option as we turn onto its narrow packed dirt.

Henry and I walk for a good hour before we hear anything that sounds remotely human.

The sun has long set by now, but the sky is still in dusk form.

I have heard there are some places where the sun never really sets. I vaguely wonder in the back of my mind if this is one of them. But now is not the time.

A voice cries out from around the corner. Definitely human. I hear footsteps but no more voices.

Motioning for Henry to wait behind me, I walk toward the bend in the trail. To my surprise, it opens into a clearing. There are guards running in circles, spinning, and crumpled on the ground.

Looking into the center of the commotion, I try to figure out what is going on. There are so many bodies I am unable to distinguish the cause of this insane pandemonium.

Whoever is fighting them from within seems to have a common enemy with me, so I decide to help. Knocking out the stragglers and preventing more from joining the fray, I notice how easily the fighter tosses out one soldier after another. This mysterious warrior is almost better than I am.

I focus on the two soldiers running from the clearing. Once I catch them and return, the cause of the scene is in full view. I watch as one last man slumps to the ground before Ash turns to see me.

"I wondered who was helping me." He says with a smile as he walks over to embrace me.

"You can't get rid of me that easily."

"Seeing that I was coming to rescue you, I wouldn't exactly say I wanted you gone." Ash glances around at the woods. "You know, if you wanted me to prove my love, you didn't have to get yourself captured and carried three kingdoms away."

"Well, it seemed like a worthy challenge for a worthy suitor."

"Personally, it felt like a worthy royal pain."

I chuckle.

Henry peeks around the corner.

Ash spots him and asks, "Shall I get him, or do you want him?"

"He's one of ours," I reply quickly.

The soldier's jacket did its job. Ash assumed Henry was a guard, just like the rest of them.

"Let's get out of here before more find us," I tell them. "Do you know where the nearest town is?"

Ash nods and calls over his shoulder, "Follow me," as he walks straight into the woods with no trail attached. I shake my head but decide to trust him as I hurry behind him into the brush.

Chapter 22

The town is quaint. People move about their own business. They look ordinary. There are no soldiers to be seen. This is not like any town I have ever been to.

We hide in the woods. If someone saw us in our current clothes, we would be in trouble. My dress is torn yet still too fancy for this quiet town, Henry wears a strange soldier's jacket, and Ash looks like he took a bath in mud.

It would not be the best idea to wander around on the streets looking like that.

I spot a tailor shop toward the edge of town. It does not appear to be very high end. In fact, it almost looks abandoned.

I ask Ash and Henry to stay in the woods. I wait until dark and then creep toward the building.

It stands alone and appears to have living quarters in the back. There are multiple trees surrounding the shop which allow me to slip unseen toward the entrance.

Two young girls play in the backyard. They have small cloth dolls for toys, the little yellow threads bouncing from the top of their heads as the girls toss their dolls around. The dolls look well-loved and obviously are carefully made.

I pull on the door gently. It creaks as it swings open. Stepping into the small shop, I see a young man walking around a dress doing measurements. He spots me as I enter.

"Shops closed," he calls brusquely from behind the dress.

"I think I have something that might be worth your while."

He stares at me for a moment. "We don't deal with your kind here."

"My kind?" I genuinely have no idea what he is talking about. How could he know who I am and if he did there would be no way he would address me in such a manner.

"Your kind. Cheap heels, a frilly dress splotched in mud and riddled with holes, a filthy peasant pretending to be someone she's not."

"I'm not a peasant." I am indignant.

He clearly has no idea who I am. But his statement about being a filthy peasant ticks me off.

"I need three individual outfits of standard dress for the people in this region," I tell him.

"It seems you didn't hear me. We don't serve your kind here. This is a respectable dress shop. It may not look like much, but I do a good job and I serve quality patrons. You need to leave. Now."

He takes a step toward me and I tense, anticipating a fight. He does not touch me but moves past and opens the door.

"Out!"

I remain facing into the room. "I repeat, I need three outfits of standard dress for this area. I will pay you well and unlike your faulty thinking, I am not a filthy peasant."

I am coming to the end of my patience. He is stubborn, but I embody stubbornness. I am relentless until the end. He will not convince me to leave this shop until he gives me what I want.

"If you don't leave now, I'll have to forcibly escort you out."

"I'd like to see you try."

I sense him turn and notice the slight tightening of his hand on my wrist. I hadn't wanted to fight but I needed to get out some of my anger.

In reality, if I ever admit it to myself, this was what I desired as soon as he called me a filthy peasant. Honestly, even before I walked into this shack, I knew I wanted one, but it took that line to make me incensed. I don't know if I've ever been so insulted.

Today has been a long day and I am ready to get what I want. My uncle betrayed me and tried to kill my best friend. My best friend followed me literally halfway across the world trying to save me. I had to fight my way out of a cell where the guards did not respect me. My favorite guard was beaten because he protected me. And, to top it all, my new favorite dress is ruined.

I am tired, worn out, and done with this. I am going to get my way.

My arm twists of its own accord, shifting his grip so that I have a better hold on him than he does on me. Yanking him in front of me, I force him over his work bench.

His nose is inches from a pair of long, sharp scissors, but he will never be able to reach them.

The shock of the young man renders him unable to respond for a moment. Once he regains his senses, he struggles lightly, soon realizes that any attempts are futile, and finally groans, "Bloody... well... I never... fine... I'll make you dresses. Just get your grubby hands off."

"You will respect me and my friends, too," I command him strictly.

"Fine."

He reminds me of a whiny kid. I release him from my hold and he straightens grouchily.

Glaring at me, he grabs a measuring tape. I ask for a piece of paper and a pencil. After he begrudgingly complies with my request, I quickly write out the measurements for myself, Ash, and Henry in neat cursive.

The young tailor stares at my handwriting a moment before picking up the paper, clearly noticing the evenness of the lines and the precision it contained. Not the scribble of a 'filthy peasant'.

"What's your name?" He finally asks.

"Rose. Yours?"

"Charles," he replies evenly. "The outfits will be done tomorrow afternoon around five."

"See you then," I say with a smile and slip out the door, but not before I see him grimace. It pains me to involve the innocent but I will pay him well.

Chapter 23

After sneaking back into the shop to pick up the two pantsuits and simple dress, Henry, Ash, and I change in the woods. I gave Charles three black diamonds for his work. Seeing that I have hundreds, I figured I could be generous. The dress and work suits both cost less than half a diamond but I was feeling kind.

While I was inside, I asked him for a saw and some rope. He procured the items. Henry and Ash had already collected trees that would be worthy of building a cabin with.

After a short talk last night, we came to the conclusion that it would be best to live here.

We are not in a registered kingdom but in an in-between area where neither kingdom is greatly interested in claiming this small strip of land. These people have no loyalties to King Samuel or my father. They will not bother us.

It takes us a week to construct a log cabin, but it is finally finished. Every day, I have asked Charles to obtain necessary food and supplies for us.

He might not claim that I asked but his choice was to comply or be tortured. He chose to comply.

***

A week passed by, then two. Before we knew it, two months had gone by. Charles regularly visited the cottage now, assisting with anything we needed. He seemed to understand that we were hiding from something but he never asked.

I spent the time in half bliss half torture. On one hand, I had Ash all to myself. No parents or uncles to separate us. No torture or imprisonment. Just us.

We spent every day together, sharing tasks, stories, and secrets. I opened up in a way I never had before. Ash was someone I trusted completely.

To place a cherry on top of his handsome features and charming character, we were an excellent team. Training with Ash allowed me something I had never experienced, an equal opponent.

We would fight every day, toning our skills and strategies. Each day held a different winner. We fought as equals.

One early morning, just as the sun cleared the horizon, we made our way into the woods. Carrying our bows, we each managed to take down two birds, a turkey, and some squirrels.

As we headed back to the cabin, Ash fell behind me. I turned to make sure he was okay, only to realize he had disappeared entirely.

I dropped my load.

Slowly, I spun in a circle. Was he captured or was he trying to attack? I hadn't heard a struggle, but the morning birds were loud and I wasn't paying attention.

A flicker of movement out of the corner of my eye and then he was upon me. We fought, each getting in a few blows. Ash went in for another punch which I raised my arm to block.

Halfway through, he twisted just enough to grab behind me, tackling me to the ground.

I landed on my back, Ash two inches from my nose, his forearm threatening to choke me. He released but did not rise.

My eyes locked on his, as if forming some sort of contract.

For the first time, Ash's dark brown gaze looked unsure, not steady. The sticky sweat piled on both our foreheads and dripped down my temple. I didn't move my hand to wipe it off.

Instead, my hand rose, brushing Ash's curly hair off his forehead. My hand didn't seem to want to leave so I left it nestled in his wavy locks.

My eyes found his mouth, lips parting. Then, he leaned in and they were on mine. Sweet with sweat, soft, and full of warmth. My heart was in my throat. Goosebumps covered my arms and legs.

His hands in my hair. Mine on his face. How long we stayed there, I don't know. My stomach grew wings and started flying, my cheeks burned red, and the only thing I knew was that I never wanted this moment to end.

Eventually, Ash pulled back, grinning from ear to ear.

"I've wanted to do that for a while," he whispered to me. Like he felt someone was going to overhear us. "I hope I didn't overstep."

I pursed my lips into a smile and instead of responding, pulled him back down, kissing him again and again.

My eyes glaze into focus, staring at the pot of water just beginning to simmer. That was my first kiss, on those pine needles under the rising sun.

I recollect on how different everything was from that day on, yet nothing really changed. Our routines stayed the same. Our meals, friendship, conversations. Everything felt normal, yet when we were in the woods, our lives changed. Ash wouldn't pull me behind a tree because he thought he heard a human. Instead, we'd climb high into an oak as he pulled me close and kissed me.

Lying in wait, I would lay curled up in his arms, watching for prey. His lips just touching my hair. I love the strength of his arms around me. The warmth of his breath just inches from my lips. The way he smiles just after we break apart, waiting for me to pull him back in, because he knows I will.

We told Henry a few days after our first kiss. He seemed to expect it, but pursed his lips nonetheless. Life continued as if nothing had changed. Ash was my happiness, my comfort, my love.

He was the half of my life that brought me joy.

The other half was consumed with my parents. Worrying about my uncle. Scared he would find me. Afraid of what he might do to my mother if he treated me this way. Anxious to see my father again.

I feel the knot in my gut tighten as I worry. My father was sick. What if he died and I never saw him again? What if he was already dead and I didn't know? Could I leave my mother to mourn by herself?

My stomach is a tortuous ball of pain, rolling from one storm to the next. Half wanting to be found and half dreading the consequences.

I roll up my sleeves and place another log on the fire.

I worry about my father. His illness only worsened when I was at the castle. I remember his smile as he would laugh. The way he picked me up and twirled me around as a little girl. The way I could tell him anything.

The homesickness builds in my chest. I miss them both terribly but what could I do to help?

My parents would never pick Ash as a suitor. I have to choose. Both cannot exist in my life. The debate begins in my head again.

Ash.

My parents.

Which one needs me more? Which do I love more? Who could I walk away from and not feel guilty for the rest of my life? These are the questions I grapple with every day. Wondering what would happen if I simply walked out the door and abandoned both.

The pot of water is boiling on the stove as Ash walks in the door. He normally rises earlier than me to get food from Charles.

I remain at the pot, dumping in mint, chocolate, and a pinch of sugar, waiting to feel his arms encircle me. Instead of the normal hug and peck on the cheek, I felt his hand on my shoulder, his lips by my ear.

"They have Charles." His whisper is barely audible.

"Where?" I reply, suddenly tensing. My disappointment at not being loved on is fighting with my fear for Charles' family.

"Hazelton guards are surrounding the house. I couldn't see inside. I left as soon as I saw it."

I want to kick myself for growing complacent. How they were led to Charles, I don't know.

But I have no doubt that it can be traced back to our actions. After not being threatened for so long, I finally thought we might be free. But I had mistaken my uncle. He would never leave me alone.

"How many?" I ask, dread welling up in the pit of my stomach.

"A couple hundred," he replies. "There were more coming from the woods as I left." I rise to wake Henry.

Ash explains the situation.

"We need to leave," Ash says, already pulling food together into a bundle and gathering our hunting weapons. "Now."

"We can't leave Charles," I interject.

"That's not an option." The voice comes from the doorway.

The three of us swing around to face Mek. He stands strong, an irritated look on his face. "So, I heard you were kidnapped." Mek doesn't ask the question, but I know it's what he wants answered.

Why didn't you come back? His eyes assail me. "My uncle hired the kidnappers."

"So?" Mek has that undeniable attitude that makes people tell him things.

I sigh. "I was worried for my safety and Ash's. Henry committed treason by trying to protect me."

My answer is enough for Mek. He can fill in the blanks.

"I've been given orders by your uncle to take you home and bring the two of them in for treason." Mek gestures to Ash and Henry with a wave of his hand, eyes never leaving my face.

I gaze at him. It wasn't a question, yet he didn't seem to demand a faithful response. "And if I say no?" I ask, tilting my head.

"I will be killed." Mek's answer, though straightforward as always, catches me off guard.

"How?" I ask. And then, "Why?"

"I will have failed in my duty."

Mek does not mess around. If he says our non-compliance will kill him, it will. I glance at Ash. Over the past two months

145

we have grown closer and closer together. I absolutely abhor the idea of leaving him. At the same time, I love Mek like a father and I would do anything to keep something bad from happening to him.

Ash holds my eyes for a moment and, as if reading my thoughts, he nods. For a moment, I wonder if I'll ever meet another person who knows me so well, who has the same sense of loyalty, the same love of country and friends, and who loves me just as much as I love him.

"I will return with you," I tell Mek resolutely, tearing my eyes from Ash and forcing the pain out of my voice. "But leave them."

He watches me for a moment. "I believe that will be enough." He nods. He sees me glance at Ash again.

"I'll give you a minute."

This is the most sensitive I've ever seen him. Mek quietly steps out and closes the door. I hug Henry first. He bids me adieu, and, knowing full well Ash is much dearer to me than he ever will be, excuses himself.

The door clicks shut behind him and I throw my arms around Ash. His arms hold me in a steady embrace and I realize I'm shaking.

"Dahlia, you're doing the right thing to save your friend," he tells me. I nod into his chest. Afraid I might start crying.

"Henry and I'll be all right," he assures me. "Don't worry about us. We'll look out for each other."

His hand cups my chin, lifting my face so I gaze directly into his dark brown eyes. "Take care of yourself, Dahlia." His gaze is searching, pleading. "Promise me."

"I promise," I tell him in a broken voice.

He leans down, lips finding mine, holding me in that close

embrace. I am suddenly aware of all I am about to lose.

The door squeaks open. We break and I turn to see Mek watching us. His features are the closest to sympathy that I have ever seen.

Not one for emotional displays, he asks brusquely, "You ready?"

I nod, glance at Ash, and walk out the door without looking back. My heart is glass and my uncle just hit it with a sledgehammer.

Chapter 24

Mek does not mention the kiss he witnessed but it is on both of our minds as we ride through the woods. He had brought a horse for me to travel on. The guards had released Charles and his family after Mek brought me to them.

At first, they resisted because Mek had not retrieved Ash and Henry.

Mek vaguely mentioned that he was unable to obtain us all and he made me his first priority. His statements left open to interpretation if I had even been with Ash and Henry.

I silently thanked Mek for his kindness. It saved me many questions that would force me to lie.

We left the soldiers to evacuate and rode ahead.

After glancing behind us, Mek looks at me expectantly. I cave.

"He's the best and only suitor I'll ever have. Please don't judge me." His eyes flicker with my words. "Mek, I love him."

I don't want to guilt him, but he needs to understand how much I'm losing. Mek has never married. Now that I think about it, I doubt he ever had a girlfriend.

"I know." The calm firmness in his voice surprises me. I glance at him questioningly, lost in my thoughts and confused about what he knows. "I saw the way you kissed him. You are close. There is no doubt about that."

I glance down. "My family will never approve."

"Your uncle might not. I would not write off the rest of your family. The Queen just wants you back. She would gladly accept you and your friend over not having you."

"But she gets me. And I had to leave Ash." Voicing that thought makes my eyes well with tears. I push them down. I don't want Mek to think I'm getting emotional.

"I'll put in a good word for him." I stare at Mek, shocked. "Or not... if you don't want—"

I cut him off, "No, please do. I just wasn't expecting you to..."

I trail off. I didn't expect him to what? Be kind? Care? Help me? How could I phrase my sentence without insulting Mek?

He smiles. "I'm not just your instructor, Dahlia. I also happen to care about my student's life."

"Well, I appreciate it," is all I can say.

"You better," he replies.

***

Ash's hands and wrists are tied with a thick rope that burns the flesh. I watch as my uncle instructs a masked soldier to hang him from the rafters in the dungeon.

My body shakes from the cold as I struggle against my captors. Faithful to the crown, these soldiers force me into a chair, tying my ankles to the legs and forcing my arms behind the back of the chair.

I try to scream but no sound comes out. Pleading, I beg them to let me go, to let me help Ash. They don't seem to hear me. A man with a long sharp knife approaches Ash. I'm glued to my chair, unable to move. There seems to be no help for Ash. I am hopeless.

The man throws back his arm and thrusts forward, impaling Ash with one lethal move.

His dark eyes blink shut as he contorts.

I wake with a gasp. Swirling around in my bed, taking in the surroundings of my familiar room. My prison. My uncle has confined me to this room since I returned.

I haven't seen my mother or Mek at all. The only human interaction I've had has been when the door slips open and a maid drops a tray of food on my floor. It immediately slides closed and I am left in solitude.

Finally, two days before my eighteenth birthday, Uncle Adkin walks through the door. I watch him from my bed, an open copy of *The Tempest* in my hands.

He sits down on the edge of the love seat, facing me.

"Are you going to kill me?" The genuine question escapes my lips before my brain has time to stop it.

My uncle quirks an eyebrow. "No." He looks confident. It scares me. "Not yet."

"Well, that's reassuring." I tell him. If he can be cockily honest, so can I. "How's Dad?" I ask.

My uncle smiles. "He's dying appropriately." I wince at his insensitive manner.

With a smug smile, he says, "After all this time, I finally get to rule while he feels the pain I've felt for years."

I bristle but remain silent, my rage and pain conflicting for control over my heart. "You know, Dahlia, I wanted for you to rule, with my guidance." He looks at me. The harsh outline of his face is stark after not seeing another human for so long. "But then I realized, I didn't need you to rule. I could rule by myself, without you."

If this exclusion is supposed to hurt me, it doesn't

succeed.

"Like I would be sick enough to let you help me rule," I spit at him, my fancy diction failing me as my brain spins. Uncle Adkin seems a little too pleased with my father's illness.

He simply smirks, "Dahlia, I don't need your help. You can rot away. But I'll always be the true king."

"And what if my father gets better?" I inquire.

"Don't worry. He won't," my uncle sneers.

I blanch. Is he implying what I think he is? Could he really be so callous to his own brother?

"You…" I stammer. "You didn't… You aren't…"

"Believe me," Uncle Adkin drawls. "I can and I will. All it takes is a few drops of poison in his daily soup bowl."

He pauses for dramatic effect while I gape at him. "That's all he can eat now anyway."

My uncle grins at me, taking in the full of my reaction.

I'm glued to my bed, stuck with my mouth gaping open like a fish gasping for water.

Uncle Adkin is poisoning my father. The thought seems to be on an icy pond, slipping around in my mind as I try to order my thoughts. A chill runs down my spine.

With that realization, my uncle grins evilly as he rises and exits the room.

Chapter 25

I'm worried sick about my mother. If my uncle can poison my father, will he go so far as to wipe out my father's entire family? Every hour of her absence frightens me more than the last.

I pick up the family picture from my bedside table. My father's face is full and happy, grinning from ear to ear as he pulls my mother and me to him. Tears well in my eyes as I think about his kindness. His heart was ours.

Now we may never see him again.

My heart jumps into my throat as I choke up, thinking of the day we took this picnic.

It was just beginning to be summer. The trees were green and everything was in full bloom. My father planned a surprise for just my mother and me. After dragging us out of the palace on the false pretense of visiting a great aunt, he took us up into the mountains.

Under the great trees singing in the wind, we made our picnic. Since we traveled on horseback, there wasn't as much food as usual, but it was much more fun.

Mother and I played chef as we sliced bread and cheese to make sandwiches. Father had brought a guitar and he played it for us. It wasn't very kingly to know how to play the guitar, but we were learning it together.

When we finished eating, my mother brought out her

sketchbook. Father and I played a game of hide and seek in the woods.

She sketched us all together that day. Father had it framed for my birthday. I can't stand the thought of losing him.

The door squeaks open with my morning breakfast. I have not slept a wink. I wait for it to close but it doesn't. Tilting my head, I see Mek standing in the doorway holding my tray.

He slides the door shut.

I take one quick glance to make sure no one else has entered before opening my mouth to warn him. To tell him everything.

"I know, Dahlia." He slides the breakfast tray onto my lap.

"Mek, you need to… Wait, what?" I sputter, unsure. Does he really know how far my uncle has stooped for power?

"Well, do something," I demand. Then, "Why haven't you done something?"

"I am loyal to the crown, not your family. When your mother gave King Adkin power, it was too late. There was nothing I could do. I cannot cross your uncle until your father regains his health."

I stare at him blankly. Mek just refused to help me. Of course, he used a lot more froufrou and multiple excuses but the essence to it was he refused this task, this mission.

"I'm sorry, Dahlia." His words reach me through a haze. "I wish there was more I could do."

With that comment, he simply rises and leaves. My eyes are still stuck to where he was sitting, shock coursing through my body. Out of the corner of my eye, I glimpse a sliver of light reflecting off metal. And I see the key fall off the chain connected to his waist and land on the carpet.

The door clicks shut.

Does he want me to use it? Did he mean to leave it? Should I use it? Will I be any help to my family if I do? Will I just make things worse?

These questions swirl around in my head as I rise from my bed and daintily pick up the small key, turning it over and over in my hands.

Mek never does anything by accident. And, for better or worse, I'm not one to sit around and let trouble come to me.

I start planning my attack.

Chapter 26

SMASH! The mint green vase crashes through the window behind me. I roll behind the sofa, hiding my head. I hear another crack as my assailant hurls two knives at me, one after the other. I duck as they sink into the Verde room's seafoam green wall behind me.

Silence, I peek around the edge of the sofa. The soldier lies dead at the foot of the desk.

An arm wraps around my waist from behind while the other hand covers my mouth. I struggle for a moment until I see the gloves. The fine leather gives me pause. The gloves belong to Mek.

My relaxation allows my assailant to swing me around. Inches from Mek's nose, he glares at me.

"I don't like killing our own guards," he hisses at me. "I gave you the key this morning to help you sneak out, not start a fight."

"I thought you said you couldn't help." I grin. "I'm so glad you changed your mind!"

With Mek by my side, I might be able to actually win this fight with my uncle. I feel a flutter of hope in my chest.

"I didn't," he grunts, releasing me and retrieving the two knives from the wall. "I can protect royals, not harm them."

My stomach sinks. So much for a little backup.

This day had already been way too long. I snuck out of

my room at ten p.m. using the key Mek gave me. The castle was dark and it wasn't long before a guard found me.

My uncle must have changed the guard patterns while I was gone.

I quickly silenced the guard and placed him in the linen closet behind the sliding door.

After sneaking around for about an hour, I realized I had no idea where my father was being kept.

Another guard found me then. That was when I slipped into the Verde room to muffle the noise down the corridor.

Now, it is almost twelve a.m. and my father is nowhere to be found. I need to keep moving.

"Where's Adkin keeping the king?" I growl at Mek. My frustration gets the best of me as I stare him down.

"I'd try the Veleno bedroom," he says, meeting my gaze. "But you didn't hear it from me."

"You know I won't hurt you for helping me."

"I know," Mek's gaze is cold. He sets the knives on the desk. "I was never here."

With that he turns around, heading for the doorway. As the door is nearly closed, his face reappears in the crack.

"I'm going to bed. I suggest you do not wake me."

I incline my head to show I understand. Mek has orders to protect royalty by rank. My uncle gets priority over me if Mek hears him. Essentially, if I wake Mek, I will have to fight them both. And that means he will have to kill me.

The door slides shut and Mek's footsteps disappear down the hall. I sink to my knees as waves of nausea roll over me. I haven't fought anyone in the three weeks I was confined to my room, and I am very rusty.

The stress in my chest tightens, threatening to choke me. My mother is alone right now. Completely at the mercy of my uncle. Her face swims before my eyes, peaceful and kind. I can't let anything happen to her.

My father, poisoned by his own brother, lies on his deathbed. I may never see him if I do not succeed.

Ash. Oh how I miss him. His soothing eyes and charming smile. The way his arms wrap around me and pull me close. His bright, joyous laugh. I wonder what toll the wilderness has taken on him. How is he holding up? Has he grieved our separation like I have? Despite imprisonment on both ends, we have not been separated for more than a week at a time.

My fingers tremble as I grasp the two knives and slide them into my belt. My clumsiness costs me a nick on my thumb. I suck on it and dry it on my pant leg.

Henry and Ash are on the run right now. If I win, I can bring them home.

Taking a deep breath to calm my nerves, I open the door and slip into the hallway.

Peeking around each corner before I commit to a hallway, I work around the guard routes as quickly as I can. The fastest path to the Veleno bedroom passes my own room.

I quietly jog down the hall, my eye on the next corner, when I notice my bedroom door is ajar. I stop in my tracks.

Who could be in my room at this time of night? If they are, they know I'm gone. So why no alarm? Where are the swarms of guards to take me away?

Maybe they just found out I was missing. If so, I need to take them out first before they sound the alarm.

I creep toward the doorway, listening for signs of an intruder.

"What have they done with her?" a voice questions. "We need to find her, *now*."

"Keep your voice down," a second person hisses.

So not only one but two need to be taken out. Our guards are well trained, but I can easily beat them. So why the secrecy? What do they have to hide? Are they supposed to kill me before my birthday?

"Maybe she's in the dungeon," the first man speculates in a slightly lowered voice. "We don't have much time. If we can't find her in the next half hour, we'll have to come back. We've already stayed too long."

"We're not leaving this castle without her," the second voice commands. Not just any second voice. Ash.

I don't hesitate. Whirling through the door, Ash and Henry look up in surprise before I collide into them.

"You came back," I whisper into their shoulders. Immediately, I pull away. My senses joining my emotions.

"What are you doing here?" I demand, glancing back and forth between the two of them. "You're dead if they find you."

"We realized we let Mek take something that wasn't his," Henry said.

"So we decided to come back and get it." Ash smirks.

"I'm not an object." I glare at them, crossing my arms. "And I went of my own accord. This is my place."

"Sure, sure," Ash says, "Let me know when you've decided to stop lying to yourself."

"How am I lying to myself?"

"This isn't your 'place'." Ash takes me by the shoulders. "Dahlia, we are. You belong with us. Just like we belong with you. And you may think you came here willingly but that was only because Prince Adkin threatened you with Mek's life. That's not a choice unless you're a horrible person."

"And you think I'm not a horrible person?"

"No, just a smidge higher than the horrible person bar."

Ash pinches his fingers together to give me a picture. "Don't worry though, you're close."

I scoff but hold his gaze as he bites his upper lip. He is so adorable and he has no idea.

Correction, he has some idea, but only because I tell him.

The tiny piece of my heart that has held together shatters as I tell him, "I can't leave." The confusion on his face is evident, as well as the hurt.

"Why?"

His voice cracks and I almost give in. But I remind myself that my family needs me. Sacrifices must be made. I cannot leave them to fight by themselves. I will see Ash again.

"I need to stop my uncle. He's poisoning my father."

It seems like such an oversimplification of the turmoil rolling around in my chest yet it encompasses everything.

Henry looks up at me sharply, "What?"

"And I thought my family was messed up," Ash mutters.

"I've got to find my uncle and stop him," I say. "But first I need to find my father and get him to give me the crown."

"But…" Ash looks confused. "He can't give you power. You're too young."

"Actually," I glance down at my watch, "I turned eighteen two minutes ago."

Ash grins at me. "Good timing."

I roll my eyes.

"So where's your father?"

They can't possibly believe that I would let them go with me. My father, even in his incapacitated state, would want Ash dead and they would both be killed if they were found. My uncle could only lock me up and call me a lunatic, unfit for the crown.

"You two need to get out before they find you."

"No," both Ash and Henry answer at the same time.

Henry glares at me. "With all due respect, *Princess Elowyn Dayana Wisteria*, you're not queen yet. I'll take orders from you when you've got the power to give them."

"Fine." So what, I could use the help. "But if you're captured, I can't help you. The king is my priority."

"Yeah, yeah." Henry smirks. "Save the speech. You're glad we're staying and we all know it."

Henry's friendly banter is enough to get me back on track. We don't have time for this. "Okay, whatever. Be quiet and follow me."

I peek out the open door. Not a single soldier came by while we were conversing. Odd. A warning flag waves in my mind but what can I do about it now?

Ash, Henry, and I make our way from hallway to hallway as quickly as possible. Finally, I lean around the last corner. My heart jumps into my throat as I yank myself back behind the wall.

There are soldiers everywhere. The hallway is packed full of them like a case of sardines. Shoulder to shoulder, one in front of another, wall to wall. There is no way I can get through them all.

Ash and Henry see my wide eyes and take a look for themselves. Henry yanks us all into the closest room.

"Stay here," he whispers.

Ash and I glance at each other; the soldiers will not obey Henry. He has been convicted of treason. What is he doing?

A second later it all makes sense.

Henry's louder than normal footsteps march away from the door and around the corner.

They stop.

"Oh," he projects. "Hello, fellas."

Then, his footsteps race back down the hallway and past the door. A thunderous stamping of feet chases after him.

As the chase fades away, I smack an open palm to my forehead. No time to worry now. I won't let Henry's sacrifice go to waste.

Ash and I slip out the door and proceed to the hallway. There are five guards left blocking the doorway.

We really need to work on priorities. Only about five guards needed to chase him, not fifty. I make a mental note to address the flaw later. If I am still alive, that is.

I walk around the corner and toward the guards. Here goes nothing. "I would like to speak with my father," I demand of the guards.

They reach for their weapons but do not draw them.

"Look," one of the guards, Bill, says. "We don't want to hurt you, but we can't let you kill the king."

"Kill the king?" I ask, appalled.

"We know you've been unstable since you were kidnapped. You need to go back to your room. It's for your own good."

Bill's voice is aimed for a small child. My uncle spread even more lies than I thought. "I'm not unstable, Bill." I try to persuade him. "My uncle is spreading lies and poisoning my father. I need to see him."

"He said you would say that," Bill says, gently reaching out and turning my arm so I am facing away from the door. "Go back to your room where it's safe."

I sigh. So much for diplomacy.

Grabbing his extended arm, I twist it behind his back and

slam his head into the wall. He collapses to the floor. Ash, seeing that my attempt to talk them into helping me didn't work, springs around the corner.

"Go." His eyes are intense. "I'll cover you."

I grab the key ring off Bill's belt and sort through them until I find the right one. Ash quickly moves between the guards and the door. There are only four of them. Easy pickings for Ash.

I fumble to fit the key in the lock and turn the knob. The door slides open. Ash, having already knocked out the remaining guards, slips inside after me. As he shuts the door and relocks it, I freeze.

The room is dimly lit but it does not disguise the emaciated body lying under the single sheet. My father is a wisp of the man he once was. His cheeks are pale and sunken. His hands, which once held me so tightly, tremble visibly. His eyes, always bright and witty, look empty and desperate. His skin is parched and tiny cracks run across it.

I move toward the bed slowly, eyes only for my father. I am hurt by his looks and repulsed. How could my uncle take such a strong man and break him like this? Especially his own brother?

My hand reaches out to touch his and he grips mine frailly. My heart is in my throat, and I am at a loss for words. As I open my mouth to speak, a body thuds to the ground behind me.

I spin around and my eyes find Ash unconscious on the floor.

Chapter 27

"Well, well, well, what have we here?" My uncle drawls from the corner. "I have to thank you. You brought the two most wanted men in the kingdom right to me. How thoughtful."

I stare at him. How was I so stupid? I should have seen him the moment I entered the room, but I let my emotions get the best of me.

"What? At a loss for words?" He chuckles. "Don't worry, I have plenty to say. You really set yourself up well, Dahlia."

He takes a step forward into the light.

"Escaping from your room, locking a guard in the linen closet, murdering another one. Then you were assisted by two convicted felons into your father's bedroom after you took out another fifty guards. And finally, right before you murdered the poor king…" He cocks his head at me, grinning, "I tried to stop you. But you would not be stopped. You, the evil, sick child that you are, plunged your dagger into the king's chest. And I, to stop you from killing anyone else, unfortunately slit your throat."

He smirks, taking a step closer.

"It is a great story, don't you think? I will have to embellish it slightly before I give the official report. Unfortunately, you will be too dead to hear it."

His smirk turns into a full grin.

"Oh, and don't worry about your precious boyfriend. I'll

make sure he receives the death he deserves: a public, painful one with lots of torture."

He pauses for dramatic effect.

"So, my dear princess, the question remains: shall I kill you first or your father? Or would you like to do the dirty deed yourself?"

I reach for the knife in my belt.

"As much as I like your story, I like mine better," I tell him, "So how 'bout you shut up."

"My poor girl," he says, "If only you weren't so demented. Kill her."

For a split second, I wonder who he thinks he's talking to. But a second person emerges from the shadows, and I become busy trying to stay alive.

Though I have fought Mek a thousand times, I have never worked so hard to try to stay out of his reach. Every move has to be sheer perfection. A single mistake doesn't mean starting over. It means death.

Prince Adkin walks over to my father and peers down at him.

"Oh, my dear brother, I do hope you're awake enough to see all this," he sneers. "It would be such a shame if you missed your only child's death. And by the very teacher you assigned her, no less."

My uncle's words reach me through the blows Mek directs at every part of my body. It is all I can do to block them. Ducking, spinning, blocking, diving. My uncle watches on as if this was sport.

"Look, brother, she's getting tired. I think he'll have her soon."

I am too preoccupied to pay close attention, but his next

sentence makes me falter.

"I think I'll put her mother's head on a stake. Say she paraded it into your room before she killed you. That'll make it easier, since no one will know the truth besides me. And what I say will be the truth, as far as *my* people are concerned."

My moment's hesitation costs me dearly. Mek forces me into a headlock, throws me against the wall beside the window, and holds a knife to my throat.

"Oh my, that was quick," my uncle chuckles. "Did I distract you, Dahlia?"

He moves beside Mek, tucking a stray hair behind my ear. His cold fingers send shivers down my spine and my desire to pull away almost wins. But I won't let him get to me. Not in my last moments. I glare at him.

"Always a feisty one. Let me know how far that gets you."

He turns toward the open window. The cool night breeze rustles his hair.

I glance down at Ash. Then, up toward my father. Finally, I look straight at Mek. All the people I love, I am about to lose.

The knife digs into my skin and a drop of blood trickles down my neck. I feel a pang in my heart and my eyes begin to water, but I will not cry. This is only goodbye for a little while.

Mek meets my eyes and gives me a sad smile, "Goodbye, Dahlia. You were the best student I ever had."

I'm not sure why but his sensitivity touches my heart and I give him a smile. "Never stop being yourself," he whispers.

Wait, what? I am about to die. He wants me to be myself for the last minute of my life?

His comment also confuses Prince Adkin, who turns from the window just as Mek lunges for him, digging the knife deep into his chest.

I watch in horror as the scene unfolds. My uncle stares down at his chest for a moment, grabs Mek by the arms, and throws himself out the window, pulling Mek with him.

"NOOOOO!" I shriek, realizing too late what my uncle's intentions are. My hands grasp empty air as I lunge toward the window and watch my beloved teacher and friend plummet to his death.

Chapter 28

"Are you okay, chérie?" My mother rests her hand on my arm.

I glance up from the tear-stained cushion I was embroidering, biting my lip to keep from sobbing. She sees my watery eyes and pulls me into a hug.

It has been a week since I regained control of Hazelton. My father is on the mend, though the doctor has told us it will take him a while. Prince Adkin's doctor has been arrested and thrown in jail.

We buried the Prince in an unmarked grave in the woods, which we then burned. He did not deserve the recognition and he inspired only hate. The land was left parched and dead, just like my uncle's short reign.

For someone who caused so much pain and destruction, it is the perfect burial method.

I break down in sobs as I remember my uncle's body laid out on the pavement. Not because I mourn his passing but because Mek lay a foot to his right.

Half of me is so angry at Mek, while the other grieves his absence. How could he have been stupid enough to let himself get pulled out that window? I should have caught him. I should have saved him. Just like he saved me.

"I miss him," I cry into my mother's shoulder.

"Shh, I know, chérie. I know," she says soothingly, running her hand through my hair. "You know grief is just love with no place to go… Dahlia, Mek was a great man. One of the finest I've ever known."

I allow myself a small smile. Mek would hate to see us like this. I can see him now.

Walking through the door, barking at me to get up and get moving, telling me that this is no way for a princess to act, handing me a bow and pushing me toward the archery range. He loved his toys, dangerous as they were.

My father's first order was about Mek's burial. Since Mek was already decorated with the highest honors a man could possibly achieve, the king ordered he be buried with the royal family. He said Mek's sacrifice deserved the burial of a king. He saved our kingdom and our family.

The service was held in the palace so my father could attend and speak. When Mek was finally placed in the ground, a small part of me was buried with him. I would miss the banter with him. The way he instructed me. His straightforward bluntness paired with his protective care.

But I know he would not want me to mope or be sad. Everyone grieves. He knew that. Eventually, Mek would want me to continue living life. He made his decision. He saved the kingdom and my life. Mek would want me to respect that. So I will.

I choke another sob into my mother's shoulder.

There is a knock on the door. Quickly, I wipe the tears off my face and straighten my dress.

It slips open and Henry limps into the room. The guards beat him up pretty badly once they caught him. His face and arms are covered in purple bruises and one arm hangs in a sling while the other holds a cane that he uses to walk.

"Your Majesties," Henry begins, "I've got some exciting news."

I give him a small smile and an encouraging nod. *Tell us.*

"The king named me the head royal guard."

His face is radiant. It is a huge honor and clearly illustrates my father's trust in Henry and his thankfulness. I know I should be ecstatic but all I can manage to say without choking is, "That's great, Henry. You deserve it."

He bows his way out of the room just as I break into a fresh round of tears. Mek was the head royal guard. I shake my head to clear it, trying to keep the tears from spilling down my cheeks. I fail miserably.

One Year Later

White silk swirls around me. Pearls hang from my neck. White diamonds from my ears. A lacy veil covers my eyes. Glass heels clink beneath my feet. My heart is afloat with happiness.

A carpet of pink petals paves the way. One step after another. A hand by my side. The other tucked in my father's arm. I glance at his face. He is beaming.

With the exception of the slight droop in one eye, nothing remains in his glowing, healthy cheeks to remind us of the poison. My mother had written to him while he was sick and in a few of her letters she had explained my friendship with Ash.

My father, who is much more forgiving than my uncle, pardoned Ash instantly and took him in as an ally to our kingdom.

They quickly became good friends, giving me doubts over who Ash liked better. But in the end, he made the right choice.

My heart is full of butterflies, but they aren't nervous ones. They want to fly down the hallway, tugging me to pull off the heels and race to my beloved.

My father and I pause before the pair of double doors that lead to the cathedral. "You ready?" he asks.

"Yes," I whisper.

And I mean it. I have never been more excited for something in my entire life.

The doors swing open, and my eyes travel up the rose

adorned path, past the heads of nobles and guards, and rest on Ash. Our eyes meet and I see he is smiling.
　　And I smile back.